The Soul of a Place

By Michael C. Demchik

Cornerstone Press
2006

Printing, collating, and binding by:
Worzalla Publishing
3535 Jefferson St.
Stevens Point, WI 54481-0307

Printing made possible by the generous
contributions of Worzalla Publishing.

This book was printed in the United States.
Library of Congress Cataloguing Number: 2006936965
ISBN 0977480240

Cover design by Joy Ratchman
Photos courtesy Michael Demchik, Stephanie Demchik,
Joy Ratchman, Eli Sagor, Peggy Farrell, and Dustin Schallert

Contact information:
Dan Dieterich, Professor of English
Tutoring and Learning Center, LRC
University of Wisconsin-Stevens Point
Stevens Point, WI 54481-3897
(715) 346-2849

Cornerstone Press
University of Wisconsin-Stevens Point
Stevens Point, Wisconsin

The Soul of a Place

Table of Contents

INTRODUCTION

Mountains shape a landscape and a people in ways that flatlands can't. I have traveled through most of the country. I've seen vistas of grass that stretched out to the horizon, where cattle constantly crop the short grass shorter. I have stared in awe at views of coulees and sage, sweet grass and junipers, incredible sunrises and sunsets that disappear in minutes, and skies full of stars and so clear that you can see the trails of dust left by meteorites. These places, some incredibly desolate, have names like Alkali, Rock Gap, Eagle Coulee. They raise an independent people, who are often quiet and of mild temperament.

In other places, I have seen oceans that stretch just as far as the seas of grass with boats leaving empty and returning with fish, crabs or oysters. These towns are populated by thick skinned, sun-weathered salts that have spent days alone with only the sound of water smacking against wood and the crackling of a radio for company.

I have also lived in the Midwest, a domesticated landscape in all directions with its vast acreages of corn and soybeans, and hogs and cattle in feedlots. It is the Corn Belt…the Breadbasket…the flatlands of the Midwest, mild people, "Minnesota nice," a people that enforce conformity without a word.

Mountain people never see a world like this.

THE ECOLOGY OF THE HILLS
AND HOLLOWS

I grew up in West Virginia. These six words say little more than latitude and longitude to many from North Dakota...or Iowa...or Kansas. Indeed, when you say West Virginia, many people completely forget their high school geography class and say, "Is that near Richmond," or "Oh, I have been to Roanoke." This sort of comment about locations in the adjacent state of Virginia always generates a grumbling response about basic geography from the less than 2 million people that reside in the hills and hollows of West Virginia. These six words, "I grew up in West Virginia;" however, say more to someone from the hollows.

THE SUNRISES, WINDS, AND RAINS

Sunrises and sunsets are fast, furious and gorgeous in the plains and prairies. In the mountains, the sunsets speak with a slight draw. The sun rises slowly. Now that I live in the prairies, I see the sunrise as I walk out with buckets of feed for the hens and broilers. The sunrise is what breaks the darkness in the morning. In the mountains, the sky is bright long before you see the sunrise. The eggs and bacon have long since been eaten, the dishes washed, dried and put away before you see the sun. The sky has been bright for hours but the ground is still dark. The shadows of the mountains make the sun rise late and set early. Some hollows only see the sun a few hours a day.

Out on the prairie, I have gotten used to the wind.. Some weeks it never stops. In the winter, the snow dances and sparkles. "Snow snakes" slither across the road. Snow piles up downwind of trees. Windmills belong here. The wind blows in predictably from the northwest most of the time. People plant rows of trees called windbreaks to protect their houses from the wind and blowing snow. They call these windbreaks "groves" and struggle long and hard to get them to grow. In the mountains, trees just happen if the cattle stay out for a few months. Not so in much of the prairie, except for a few weedy trees like boxelder and Chinese elm.

In the mountains, the winds blow up the hollows in the morning and down at night. Or maybe it is the other way around; I have been gone long enough that I just can't remember for sure. This doesn't happen every day, but often enough that places get names like "Windy Hollow." I have long since forgotten this happens. It has something to do with differential heating. I remember that much from a Climatology class in college. While the prairie gets the normal winds driven by weather patterns, they are not spooky and do not chill your soul like those cold winds blowing down a hollow. They chill you deep and feel ghostly. Stories have been told for years about Confederate soldiers, murdered lovers, or angry lonely people whose wandering souls drive these winds. These stories are strangely more easily remembered than the effects of differential heating; and possibly more easily believed.

Even the rains aren't the same. Out on the edge of the prairie, we have fairly predictable patterns of rain and snow. You can draw lines called "isolines" that show a slowly increasing amount of rain as you follow the winds from west to east across Minnesota.

22 inches...23 inches...24 inches...A nice...predictable...linear pattern...very Minnesotan. But in the mountains, towns can be 10 or 20 miles apart and get huge differences in rain. The town of Pickens gets OVER 100 inches of rain a year, while the town of Upper Tract averages about 33. They are separated by less than 50 miles as the crow flies. This is the rain shadow. As the air rises up the mountain, all of the water gets "squeezed out" as the air "orographically" cools. On the other side of the mountain, the soil is dry even though you can smell the cloud burst from 10 miles away. Prickly pear cactus, not unlike what I have seen in the dry western Plains, grows in these rain shadows on droughty soils. Twenty miles away, rhododendrons bloom in the moist soils by trout streams.

WILDCRAFTERS

Differences in the rains and the elevations and the soils breed incredibly diverse plant communities. You can find botanicals and herbal medicines nearly everywhere you look. Plants with bioactivity are the dominant ground cover over many of the rich soils in the state. Some are extremely economically valuable and some are worth little money. When Daniel Boone was "out west" hunting in "Kentuck" and bagging bears at three years old, or so the story goes, he was also digging ginseng. Around 1716, a missionary in Canada read an article about a rare Asian plant in the Proceedings of the Royal Philosophical Society. This missionary, who worked with the Native Americans, guessed that this plant might live in North America. He asked the members of the bands he worked with if they knew about this plant. They confirmed that it grew here (actually, a close relative of Asian ginseng). So began the American ginseng industry.

About 50 years later, Daniel Boone capitalized on the new, undug ground in Kentuck. In 1769, Boone was the first documented European to set foot in Kentuck. Within a few years he shipped TONS of ginseng to China. A hundred or more roots might be needed to make a dry pound. A quarter to a half-million roots may be needed for one ton. Boone once flipped a canoe carrying two tons of roots, loosing the whole cargo. That is a lot of plants. I grew up in Boone County, WV, not too far from Seng Creek. The county's namesake was a 'sang digger. He may have been known as a hunter, explorer, or fighter, but first and foremost, he was a gatherer. He was definitely one of ours.

I have only seen one other place as rich in medicinal plants as my mountains: the White Earth Indian Reservation in Minnesota. Jutting out into the prairie, sugar maples live in the western-most edge of their range. A small elevational change and a bit more snowfall may contribute to the very diverse plant community that exists in the area. Historical glaciations, soil parent materials, and management by Native Americans have played a part in making a landscape so rich in botanicals. This site has soils that support the gift of medicines. The Native Americans in these bands learned to use the plants through an oral tradition and through what they learned from dreams. While in the modern world, a capsule or a bottle of pills supposedly provides relief of all that ails, the place of dreams is underestimated or forgotten. Some at White Earth, have not forgotten and neither have a few from the hollows in West Virginia. European culture has come up with a word- Ethnobotany- to describe aboriginal use of plants. Ethnobotany serves partly to record these uses being forgotten in our modern world. But ghosts and stories in books do not replace the power of the tastes, smells, and sounds. And $16.95 at the pharmacy does not replace the spiritual loss of the power of dreams in medicine.

WHERE CURVED LAND MEETS STRAIGHT LINES

The roads in the Midwest are straight and square. After the land was stolen from the natives already living there, the government set out to fill the land with settlers. When the land was surveyed, the government surveyors created six mile by six mile townships. These townships were divided into one by one mile sections. A section is 640 acres. These sections were subdivided into quarters of 160 acres; and from there into quarters of quarters also called 40's and so forth. As an example, a farmer may own Section 16 of T34N R8E, a unique number assigned to each township in the country based on location, in this case in Harrison, WI. Or he might own the "southwest quarter of the southwest quarter of the southwest quarter of Section 16," which translates to 10 acres, the legal description of some land that I own in Minnesota. Oh, are the property boundaries in the hills and hollows different from this. A property may be advertised as "40 acres MOL (more or less)" and turn out to be 75 acres or only 20 acres. The property may legally have a meander line on a stream. This stream may change course and change the property line. A fellow I knew in Boone County was doing what he called "land reclamation." He said that he had read about it in National Geographic. Essentially, he planted shrubs along his meander boundary. When the stream flooded (flash floods are a common occurrence due to the steep slopes), old logs, parts of old cars, etc. would catch in the shrubs. This material would catch sediment from the stream and make more land, on which he planted more shrubs. When I left, it seemed to be working. The old boundaries might follow old fence lines or end at corners "3 feet from the big black oak," which is now a rotten stump. As hard as it might be to believe, a portion of the Eastern Panhandle of West Virginia, not more that 100 miles from the Megalopolis that includes the nation's capital, had never actually been surveyed until the late 1980's/early 1990's. The site was simply too steep. Despite this startling imprecision, especially when one considers that these are political boundaries, mountain boundaries are usually meaningful and often logical and obvious. And while not particularly accurate (at least historically, surveys on land sales will shortly eliminate any of the inaccuracy that had existed), they are also not particularly arbitrary. Prairie boundaries are precise and silly at the same time because they are imaginary lines drawn across seas of corn and beans. Fences may be off by a foot or two, but the fence is wrong and the imaginary line is right. Precise, straight lines drawn across land that curves and bends. These imaginary boundaries are precise, yet neither logical nor obvious. All I can say is that this really fits the flatlands perfectly.

Any mountain driver knows that the land is not straight but instead curves and bends. West Virginia is noted for its switchbacks, sharp curves where the road literally changes direction so sharply that you point your car in the direction from which you came when you have completed the turn. Switchbacks exist because many of the slopes are so steep that you would literally have to climb darn near straight up in the air otherwise. Instead, you attack the hill at an angle and drive 7 miles (primarily parallel to the slope) instead of driving half a mile straight up. All in all, this works much better than buying a Volkswagen Jetta with a 5000 horsepower engine to climb straight up the slope. The popular term for this type of turn is a "kiss-me-ass turn." While all school children are scared during their first bus ride, mountain school children get to look out their bus window straight down a hill and not see any road. As the buses negotiate these roads, the wheels firmly touch the road, but the sides of the bus are suspended in mid-air over the sides of the slope. That scared the "ba-geese-es" out of me as a child. In junior high school, one of the roads we drove every day to get to school was named "Bolt Mountain Road." When you think of the name, think of a "machine bolt" not of some family called the "Bolts." Those that are not from the hills and hollows often joke that when you ask for directions in West Virginia, the locals will as often as not, say that "you can't get there from here". In many cases, this is not far from true.

MOUNTAIN DIRECTIONS

When I moved to my prairie home, it was for a job that required a great deal of driving. For the first year, I had a hard time understanding directions. People would call roads by "numbers" or even worse "letters" and say south and east. Where I grew up, while the signs had south and east written on them, you constantly switched between driving south and east… and north and west for that matter. So you seldom included the compass point in the direction. One road that I used to drive regularly out of Parsons, WV was both a north and a south route going the same direction up and over the mountain. If you take Route 72 north you also take Route 219 south, if I remember the numbers right (remember, roads are seldom called by number there). The only roads in the mountains that anyone called by numbers were interstates and even then they'd usually say, "Well, after you get onto Fox Hollow road, go 'till you get to a big, old black oak tree with a branch cut off. If you see beef cattle in the field, you went too far. Turn right and go up the hollow. That'll take you to the interstate. You can figure it out from there." In my prairie home, however, they use road numbers and talk in section lines. A typical direction might go like this, "You go out here and follow 36 south out to 54. Go east on 54 until you get to one of the section roads, then go south. When you get to route A, its also called GG, go east for about a mile. At the stop sign, go south…." My brain was programmed to see black oaks with limbs cut off, thinking in section lines and squares took some time.

MOUNTAIN STREAMS AND HUNGRY TROUT

In my prairie home, water flows lazily to the Gulf of Mexico. If I drive a few miles west, it flows lazily to the Hudson Bay, often over mud bottoms. Not so in the mountains. The water may end up in the same place, the Gulf of Mexico, but it takes on a different pace. It rushes from many tiny creeks, through numerous Army Corp of Engineers projects, to the Ohio River, then the same Mississippi, then to the same Gulf of Mexico, but it is different. This water has far more pizzazz. Cold mountain streams flow over rocks, through forests and past rhododendrons. The approach is fast. The water is clean, actually too clean. Some of these streams only have 2 or 3 pounds of fish per surface acre, often mostly brook trout. Many of the waters by my prairie home have 100 times this amount of fish. Most of the nutrients in these streams are in fish and insect biomass. If you have ever heard anyone say that they were living off the fat of the land, then these are water bodies that are skinny, nearly no fat at all. Leaves and logs feed insects indirectly or directly and these insects, in turn, feed fish. A seven inch mountain trout, on some waters, is a trophy. It might take that fish five years or more to get that big. Four-inch fish may have fall spawning colors. On rich waters, these same fish can weigh several pounds.

Fishing for these little aquatic banty roosters is great fun. Some western rivers are surrounded by grass and fly fishers love to do long, beautiful casts. By comparison, I learned to fly fish on streams surrounded by trees and over-topped by rhododendrons. I would cast in a two foot wide by one foot tall tunnel of open air above the stream and below the plants, while balancing on a half-sunken log over ice-cold water. The experience is very different. In western waters, finicky huge trout let flies drift by. In my mountain waters, these trout are HUNGRY and aggressive. I have had mis-casts with flies landing at the edge of the water, but fully on dry land. Trout have pushed their mouths up on the shore to pick up my offering. Mis-casts that I have hung in the rhododendrons will occasionally induce a trout to jump several inches above the water to grab the tasty tidbit only to be impaled on the hook and left hanging in mid-air. The old Scotch-Irish that settled this area used to fish with their hands by working them around the rocks until they found a fish to grab. I often wonder if the fish did not try to eat these fellows first. I usually release all of the trout I catch in these small mountain streams because there are so few per acre and because they are too aggressive for their own good; however, there is a bit of an exception to this rule. If I happen to come across a wild apple tree with ripe fruit, a fairly common occurrence along these highland streams, I always keep a couple of fish. Native trout and wild apples cooked in butter (especially if cooked over a wood fire) is one of the most delicious meals to come out of the mountains and would make any Savoyard proud.

RAMPS, BUCKWHEAT AND TERRIOR

The French concept of Terrior, used to sell wines of special quality, really applies to native cuisine everywhere. Terrior, in essence, means that the soil, air, temperature, and everything else that makes up a place, influences the flavor of the wine because it affects the basic nature of the product. In order to understand this concept, we really have to step back a few years to a time before tractor-trailers brought iceberg lettuce from California to the mountain markets.

My neighbors in my prairie home eat what one would call standard American fare. Hamburgers, hotdogs, macaroni and cheese…fast food, junk food, and zap-a-pack type meals. If they want to eat "healthy," maybe they will have an iceberg lettuce salad with carrots, radishes and boiled eggs. In the past they ate differently, but I was not here to know. The original settlers ate lutefisk (a holiday fish meal prepared with lye), lefse (a potato crepe/tortilla), pickled pork products and sauerkraut during the long winters. The Native Americans depended on wild rice, fry bread, meats, fish, maple sugar and dried fruits during the winters. In summer, both the Native Americans' and the settlers' diets probably varied more. The cuisine of this place was tied to the winds, winters, and people. Look at the wild rice. The terrior of this wild rice is taken from the slowly flowing water, the flails knocking the rice into canoes and the smell of the grains parched over an open fire. It is harder, and scarier, to define the terrior of a hotdog on a white bun.

When I grew up in West Virginia, the state was changing. Families still walked with buckets down the roads to pick berries; some dug ramps (a type of wild leek) and hunted morels (which they called mollymochers) in spring; they still canned apples and tomatoes each fall; and, squirrel pot pie and venison stew were not only found on the Beverly Hillbillies. We also had macaroni and cheese, frozen TV dinners and Coca-Cola.

The world was changing. Traditional foods in the mountains were based on what people could grow, gather, catch or shoot, even into relatively recent years. Thin mountain soils still could grow corn and gardens. From those that lived in midslopes and the small valleys, we got beans and cornbread. Those that left the state craved the tastes of beans and cornbread. And while store-bought beans may work, cornmeal bought in the city does not. You need to use fresh (not old and rancid) cornmeal, preferably stone-ground. Most mom and pop stores carried good cornmeal, but the chain stores usually do not now. The cornbread you make with this half rancid cornmeal just does not taste right.

If you lived really high up in the mountains, then buckwheat substituted for corn. Every year, Preston County still celebrates a festival for the buckwheat harvest, even though the buckwheat is now shipped in from New York (locals have stopped planting buckwheat due to an overpopulation of deer). For the uninitiated, a buckwheat cake is just another pancake. To someone from the mountains (and this applies to the mountains in France and Spain as much as it does in West Virginia), a buckwheat cake can be comfort food. Thin, yeast leavened crepes are cooked over extremely high heat. They are not unlike Breton Crepes. At the festival, they are eaten with whole hog sausage from pigs grown just for the purpose. To taste buckwheat cakes is to taste the mountains.

West Virginia was one of the last states in the nation to modernize. Many of the older generation fought modern ways until they died. The old foods went last in the battle. The advent of television and easy transportation out of the hollows changed that. I was born early enough to see what it used to be like but too late to live more than a part of it. Typically, if a mountain person had an intact family (often limited by fighting, marital problems and drunkenness), he or she usually had plenty of food. Even a hundred years back, when the people were emerging from the hollows to work the coal mines, going hungry for long was never considered possible. Food surrounded them in the hills and hollows. Most could get by on a garden, a corn patch, some hens and what nature provided. In town, especially coal towns, it was not quite that simple.

Across the state, I have eaten novelties that remain from of a culture that has nearly passed on. Hard cured hams and bacons that can hang from a basement ceiling for months and only get better; salt-cured green beans and sauerkraut; "cold-pack" canned deer meat; hard apple cider and freeze concentrated applejack; buckwheat cakes served with whole hog sausage; grated corn fritters; squirrel, raccoon, ground hog and venison in any of a hundred ways; ramps cooked in every savory dish there is; poke greens with vinegar; cornbread and beans (maybe the state dish); and the list goes on. In the hills and hollows, humanity's place in the food chain contrasted starkly with much of the rest of the country. For these people, the concept of terroir—although unknown—was still blooming.

As these old people die (and most already have), few will remember how the old foods taste and even fewer will know how to make them. I still make many of these things and I am still evolving them from what I have learned from people and books from the mountains in France, Spain and Italy. I want my youngsters to know how to raise chickens, how to dig potatoes; how to cure hams, how to ferment cider, and how to love their food. But these habits and this knowledge will probably die when I do. With the availability of cereal bars, chicken nuggets, and frozen French fries, maybe these things are out of place in this modern world anyway. Not fitting into the culture is a dreadful thing for a child. The need to preserve some of our cultural history through action while still being able to participate in the world is a balancing act.

STORYTELLING

My prairie home and my mountain home are full of the influences of television. Television, in many ways, has replaced the role of the storyteller. I know nothing about the roles of storytelling to the settlers in my prairie home; but I do know of its roles with the Ojibwa culture (one of the major groups of Native Americans of the Lake States). Winter was the time of storytelling. Minnesota has a VERY long winter. It starts early and it ends late. Stories were owned and were passed on as property. Most illustrated points about human nature or the environment. This oral history brought the old and the young together. It allowed the cumulative knowledge of the culture to be passed on in an exciting way.

Storytelling was much the same in my mountains. The purpose of stories in the hills and hollows was part entertainment, part education and part acculturation. Some of these "bullshit sessions," as they are often called, could go on for many hours. I really miss sitting and listening to these stories. I have adopted the role of the storyteller in my family, but listening is more fun. Born late to the mountains, I grew up with television, but its influence was much more limited than today. Today the average child watches more than 30 hours of television a week. That is nearly a full-time job which limits contact between the children and their elders. Television is the new storyteller. But this storyteller weaves different webs and acculturates children to a disconnected, homogenous and often soulless view of society. I have adopted the role of storyteller for my family and I have killed the television.

LOSING THE MOUNTAIN

A couple of years ago, a cougar was shot in Aitkin County, Minnesota. It tried to break in through the door of a house. After several attempts to repel it, the owner fearing for his safety, shot it through the door. The animal was probably a western cougar migrating east or an unwanted pet released to fend on its own. Unfortunately for me, the day before, a "cougar" was sighted on the research farm where I worked, about 60 miles from Aitkin County. I went out and looked at the tracks of the supposed "cougar." They were bobcat tracks.

They were too small and the sides of the back pads too straight to be cougars. I told my colleagues this and 24 hours later, the news of the cougar shooting hit. Credibility is a delicate thing.

Everyone wants to believe that these mysterious cats reside near their homes. Nowhere is this more evident than in the mountains of West Virginia where their existence could be true. Too many people who spend their whole lives in the woods - loggers, obsessive hunters, trappers - have seen them. After one of these people makes a cougar sighting public, they become the instant object of ridicule. I would think twice myself about reporting a sighting. A cougar was shot in my mountains in the 1970's. A cougar kitten was hit by a car in a neighboring state. And the mountains, the native home and perfect habitat for these creatures, seem much emptier without them. I hope they exist there but have no doubt that if the sightings were confirmed that some people would want them destroyed out of fear. If sightings go unconfirmed, few people would want to be known for trying to destroy a mythical creature. If there are cougars in those mountains, I hope the biologists never find them.

In this modern world, my mountains are really no different than anywhere else. Maybe more economically depressed and violent, but not really different. In some not too distant past, though, these mountains were special. When Americans think of environmental preservation, they think of old growth forests and endangered species. Because these things are at a distance and in limited supply, we value them. We have developed a society that has flourished through the systematic destruction of these things. We have separated ourselves so far from nature that we crave these special places and these special species as a way to stay connected. Without them, we feel emptier.

In my mountain home, this lack of connection was just not in the people, at least at one time. The people that lived there saw conservation through use and knew biology through practical experience. They did not have this emptiness inside themselves. They killed out these cougars and they dug up most of the ginseng. This was part of building their world. These people were more superstitious and more spiritual and more in touch with the world they found...and the world they created. It was impossible to talk about the person without talking about the place. When I look at the children and the parents now, I am surprised how much of this connectedness is gone now. While the changes in the mountains started long before my birth and will continue after my death, much of this loss happened during the short span of my lifetime.

The mountains shaped the culture more than anything else. But the culture is being forgotten and increasingly its replacement does not nourish the body or soul. I remember reading in one of the "Into Their Labors Trilogy" by John Berger, of a character who continued to plant and graft apples. His children would most likely never live on his farm. The apple trees that were on his farm would last for the rest of his life. There was no direct benefit to him or his family to plant these trees. All of the neighbors had given up on planting the trees because they felt it was a waste of time. Yet, every year the character planted and grafted new trees. Why? This character planted the trees so that his children could see and learn. If the children did not see and never used these skills, he planted them so that his ancestors would know that he had not forgotten. As with the cougars absent from the mountains, without planting these trees, something is just missing, the soul of the place is emptier.

With my family, I know that my children will know at least some of what it is like because I still "plant the trees." While my little ones know the smell of fresh cider, the taste of buckwheat cakes, and the sound of hens scratching, I doubt that their youngsters will. And without these connection or ones like them, they will have an emptiness that they won't understand. I worry about what will fill that emptiness.

My Mountains

Old Foundations and Abandoned Farms

The Wind Whistled

The wind whistled
Through walls long without people

Inside,
Squirrels and field mice den, live and die
Unknown to people
They pass their lives

From under the house,
A spring flows,
Through the stone foundation
And down the hill to the stream,
Brook trout, like brightly-colored banty roosters,
Vie for females in the shade of the walls.

The remains of a garden,
Where roses, grapes, and butternuts still cling to life
Fragrant with blossoms in spring,
Heavy with grapes and hips in fall,
Carpets of nuts in some years, none in others
Feed only squirrels and grouse,
Where people had once eaten.

Up the hill,
An apple tree, one of probably a hundred long dead
Lives from the care of years past
A skeleton for years, it still bears fruit.

Further up the hill,
An old cemetery,
Filled with carved stones, the names
Barely visible now,
And field stones placed to mark the bodies
Of souls too young for names.

This old place,
Reverting to trees,
Clumps of maples, scrawny oaks and locust,
Had births and lives and deaths,
In this place,
Mothers helped their babies take first steps,
And pulled carrots in the fall.

In another 100 years,
The walls will be gone,
The apples, roses, and grapes will have passed,
And only a few moved stones,
Some misshapen trees
And maybe some furrows or gullies
Will be all that remains to remind us anyone ever lived
here.

Does it matter that
The elements erase much of what two hands can do?
Time erases all the joy, work, pains, and fights,
After this what is left?
A shadow or a memory of some long-past struggle.

For us,
All that is left is what is now,
And what will be for us in the future,

It is important to enjoy this life because,
To waste this time,
Will matter to no one but us,
In time, a wasted life will be as forgotten as one
well-spent.

The West Virginia mountains are full of ghosts. While I mean this figuratively, many people will say that they contain actual ghosts. Walks through some mountain valleys will reveal the remains of old fields, stone foundations, and the bones of old apple orchards. These are the ghosts of long abandoned farms.

One of my favorite places to "go up on the mountain," when I lived in West Virginia, was the remains of an old farm in Preston Country. I discovered this place while following a little brook trout stream up to its source. Many trout streams in this part of the state go below ground (at least for part of the year) for a few hundred yards before resurfacing down slope. If you follow these streams upslope, it often pays to follow the underground streambed a bit further than what looks like the end. Most people don't fish the true upper limits of these streams, and they can be full of trout. This stream, however, just ended in a glade where I found the old farm.

This property now stands within a state forest and is open for hiking. It does not differ from hundreds of other old abandoned farms. During the depression in the 1930s and even many years before, people abandoned these "marginal farms" for a "better life" in the cities. Or they were taken for taxes. It was hard to eke out a living on these poor, ancient mountain soils, especially during the depression. In many parts of the state, these economic hard times still remain, making West Virginia's main export its young people. I am one of them.

This old farm, now not much more than some stone work and a few trees, must have prospered in its time. The foundation for the barn was huge. The house easily had a footprint of 1,000 square feet (probably 2,000 if it had a loft or second story). Even now, this patch of forest lies off the beaten track. One hundred years ago, it must have taken a full day or more to haul products to market. Why was the house so big? Did they have twenty kids or a big extended family? I have talked to local historians, and no one seems to know about the place. I suppose I could have gone back through tax records, but I never took the time. I doubt that this knowledge really would have meant much to me anyway. You can't tell much about who people are by their name.

THE GLADE

There was a glade down the hill below the house. Glades are patches of open, boggy ground in forests. In West Virginia, our glades are usually wet meadows. This glade had an old bucket well that was only about five feet deep. It was lined with rocks and had a short lip along the top. I never saw it without water.

This glade was mostly tall grasses and sedges with a few willows and Spirea as well as a huge patch of bedstraw. Bedstraw is a plant that has little spiny hooks along its main stem. When I was a kid, I used to delight in throwing clumps of this plant at other kids and watching it stick to them like wild Velcro. I have little doubt that if this family had children, and they almost certainly did, that the ancestors of these bedstraw plants spent a lot of time flying around this glade.

One other strange thing about this glade was that a huge balsam poplar (a tree normally considered to be a northern wetland species) grew along one side of it. Its roots were sprouting into a small balsam forest. Balsam poplars are extremely uncommon in West Virginia. This is within the natural range of the species, but nearly none of them exist in the state. I wonder what strange chain of events put this tree here. Someone must have planted or intentionally preserved it. Most of the surrounding trees are much younger and probably grew into abandoned pasture and fields. What about this tree made it special? Did it just strike someone's fancy? Balsam poplars are a medicinal plant which could explain its presence? Whatever the reason, that tree is now spreading over the glade, and that past decision has left a seed source for a locally rare tree.

THE LANE AND CEMETARY

This family must have enjoyed trees because they planted others. I noticed some sugar maples only because they looked so strange. They were obviously open grown. They had big canopies with large, low branches unlike trees that grow in forests that have to compete for light. Forest grown trees have a small crown of leaves up high and tall, straight trunks. To make it even more interesting, these sugar maples grew in two parallel rows up the slope behind the house. Most of the surrounding woods in the area consist of red maple and oaks, so these sugar maples would stand out anyway. The straight rows and open growth make them really stand out.

Why would they have planted sugar maples? Sugar maples take a very long time to grow, and these rows would most likely have run through pasture. Keeping the cattle from eating these trees would have been a challenge at best. The best answer that I could come up with was that it was either a planting for an old farm lane or a potential sugarbush for syrup. Yet another mystery.

If you follow the sugar maples up the hill and hang a left, you will find the family's cemetery. This cemetery only had a couple of dozen stones in it. The large ones bore carved names, long since worn away. I tried to do a rubbing to see if I could read the name. I covered the place the name should be with a sheet of paper and rubbed charcoal over it. I could decipher nothing. The names were too far gone. Most of the stones were little ones, field stones with no names. I have heard old-timers say that babies were not named until they reached one year old. So many of the little ones died that it saved the family grief to leave them nameless until they knew the children would survive. While I doubt that this eased the pain of a child's death, this cemetery stands as a testament to the fact that they tried.

ROSES AND APPLES

If you follow this hill around, you will find the skeletons of an old apple orchard. The few trees that remain are not much more than bleached bones. Apple trees are a strange organism. They may live for more than a hundred years. At that age, they start to decline, but they just refuse to give up the ghost. I have eaten apples from wild trees, or trees gone wild, that had one live branch on a gnarled, twisted carcass with twenty or thirty leaves and several fruits. At most, the trees on this site bear a few dozen apples a year each. These apples are usually scabby. More than half of them have worms; however, they taste great right off of the tree.

The strange thing about wild apples is when you pick them right off the tree and eat them, they taste great. After you pack them up and take them home, they're still good, but not nearly as good.

Not too far from these apples is a single rose plant, long since gone wild. That lone rose is fighting a losing battle. The surrounding trees are growing over it. Every year, most of the leaves get eaten by deer. I haven't been back since I moved to my prairie home. It may be gone already. However, this rose managed to put out a few blooms every year. I wish I had taken cuttings from this really tough rose.

These wild things are about all that remains of this place. Maybe the descendants live down in the valley or in Ohio or Maryland, the two states where most of West Virginia's economic refugees go. Maybe they have heard grandma's stories about when she lived up on the mountain. Maybe they haven't. As likely as not, nary a shadow of a memory of this farm or the family exists. All that remains is a bunch of ghosts up on the mountain.

Wild Apples

A carelessly thrown core
Or a remnant of an old orchard
Wild apples on the roadsides and trails
Bearing fruit without labor.

Ancient branches and young stems
From the same trunk
Gnarling and aging
Trees that are dying and being reborn.

Resilient immigrant
Brought by the hands of others
Finding the mountains
Calling them home.

While not native to the Mountain State, apples sure have adapted well. Wild apples are an ever-present part of the ecosystem. If a carelessly tossed apple core finds a willing patch of ground, a new apple tree is well on its way. Many thousands of wild apples start just like this every year because roadsides and hiking paths are often loaded with young apple trees.

Apples provided just about the perfect crop for many of West Virginia's self-sufficient farms. Every old farmstead had an acre or two for family consumption. After the trees were planted and established, they required little care to get a crop for HOME USE. Without any pruning, fertilizer, lime, or irrigation, they can still often produce a crop on rocky and dry soils, something that most other crops could not do. While commercial apple production is a highly managed, intensive business, home orchards were often very low intensity and may have only involved harvest after the trees took hold. Often, dairy cows or sheep grazed among the trees. This gave the animals shade. They, in turn, controlled the weeds in the orchard. The yields from such systems may have been huge when compared to the effort involved.

The tree's versatility made it truly a miracle. Apples were stored fresh and dried; they could be turned to fresh cider, then hard cider, and then either to vinegar or applejack (freeze concentrated apple liquor). The scraps of cider making could be fed to hogs. When the trees grew old, the wood was great for smoking meats. In the form of vinegar, they had a disinfectant, a cleaner, a flavoring, and a preservative for other foods. It is hard to find a more useful tree.

When I lived in West Virginia, I would camp with my wife and sometimes my stepdaughter fifteen or twenty times a year. One of my most frequented spots lay along a little mountain stream on the way to Spruce Knob not too far past a little town called Whitmer on a gravel Forest Service (FS) Road. The town of Whitmer is just a collection of houses and a small store. The little country store sells a few necessities and, at least used to, sell some delicious hard-cured bacon. If the store was open when I drove past, I used to buy some bacon for the meals. Few places still sell old style bacon anymore, so this became a ritual.

Further up the mountain, the remains of an old FS road provided a good parking spot. We'd park and follow a trail by a little mountain stream up the hillside. This trail followed the meanders of the stream with mountains on both sides. Hemlocks, birch, and rhododendrons hung over the stream and northern hardwoods covered the slopes. Northern hardwoods in the area consist primarily of sugar maple, yellow birch, beech, and an occasional ash tree in the swales.

In spring, wildflowers covered the hills. Red and white trilliums blanketed patches of the forest floor. The red ones, called Wake Robins, were more sparsely distributed, and while beautiful, had the horrid smell of rotten meat. This attracts their primary pollinators, flies, but doesn't seem to match the appearance of the plant. Other flowers with color-ful names like, Dutchmen's britches, blood root, and mayapple covered the hillslopes. When the trees have yet to fill their leaves, these spring ephemerals rise, flower, and go to sleep, before most of the trees have awakened from their long winter's nap.

Less than a mile up this trail on an old sandbar by the stream grew several wild apples. I doubt that these were intentionally planted. This part of the mountain is too steep to have been considered farm land. Even if it had, these trees are far younger than the second-growth forest that surrounds them. Most likely a hunter or a hiker pitched an apple core down on the sandbar. Maybe a deer or raccoon passed some seeds from apples they had eaten in a home orchard down in the narrow valley along the FS road. However they got here, this sandbar provided a good spot to grow. The fresh sand kept the soil weed free and it was well watered. The trees grew wild and every year at least one of them bore fruit.

Apples growing wild usually don't bear fruit

every year. They bear bumper crops, some years, and very sparse crops others. This spot is probably even harder to bear fruit in. Because this little sandbar is high up in the mountains, the weather is unpredictable. I have camped less than 300 yards from this spot and experienced a frost…in August. Apples are wonderful, productive trees, but have an Achilles Heel—late spring frosts. After the flowers have emerged, a hard frost can nearly eliminate production for that year. Along this stream, hard late frosts occur usually several times a year. However, one of these trees still bears fruit every year. And they are delicious.

One factor that I have not mentioned about this little mountain stream, is that it teams with native brook trout. Water cascades down the steep slope through boulders and downed trees, between short, deep pools and digger ponds to small waterfalls below. Digger ponds are small ponds created by the power of falling water below water falls. They usually are deep right below the water fall with a bowl shape and a lip of sand on the downstream end. They usually hold one nice trout…by mountain standards. Mountain trout on these streams are usually less than nine inches long, and typically, that is a trophy fish. The flavor and texture of these trout is much closer to Atlantic salmon and bears NO resemblance to hatchery raised trout or the trout from large rivers. These fish eat only insects. These insects eat either the tree wood or leaves. These fish are unique…the distilled flavor of water, forest, and soil.

A trout per person, a bandana full of wild apples, and the hard-cured bacon make a meal of no comparison; you are eating part of the mountains.

Stone Fences and Split Rail Worms

One thousand pounds per foot,
That is what I figure the fence weighs
Over two thousand feet long
It runs along the edge of the woods and pasture

Two million pounds of rock
Wrenched from the field
Make a pasture and fence
Out of rocky open ground

Like ten rail cars of rock
Hauled by hand and horse cart
How long did it take
To domesticate this field?

I learned a new phrase recently: inter-generational assets. This refers to money/property/training/education that is passed between generations. Good fences can be a wonderful intergenerational asset. A well-built stone fence is more than a lifelong investment. It will outlive many, many generations, and will continue to function if given periodic maintenance. A worm fence built from rot resistant woods can go more than 100 years, potentially being used by five generations with only periodic replacement of damaged rails. A well placed fence will permanently mark a property boundary, keep in livestock and keep out varmints. It becomes an item of economic value that outlives the generation that built it: an intergenerational asset.

In Dekalb, Iowa, the year 1873 is pretty important in the history of the United States because a fellow named Henry Rose took his invention to the county fair. His invention was simple: boards with nails driven through them. These nails kept cattle from rubbing a fence. Thus began barbed wire. Within a couple of years, many dozens of different designs (and the associated patent fights) emerged from this basic idea. Barbed wire is a very simple invention, at least by today's standards, but it changed the history of the world.

Imagine the Great Plains without wheat. Growing wheat without fencing out the cattle was impossible. Imagine railroads littered with dead cattle (thousands were killed every year by trains). Fencing out the cattle reduced train damage and saved millions of dollars in livestock losses. With fencing, common resources like range land could be turned into private property. Barbed wire changed the world. And it also severely limited the construction of stone and worm fences.

A three foot wide and four foot tall stone fence topped with a couple of split rails, a common West Virginia design, is an imposing obstacle. A quarter mile of this fence made with limestone could easily weigh in at 1.4 million pounds. A quarter mile of stone fence would surround about 2.5 acres: about enough to keep a dairy cow or a dozen sheep. Of course, there is some efficiency in scale, the longer the fence and the squarer the field, the more efficient the area enclosed. This is still a lot of fence and an awful lot of work. How many weeks or months of time does it take to build a fence like this for one dairy cow?

To build this same fence as a split rail worm would take something like 900-1000 rails. Figuring that a good rail splitter could do 200-300 rails a day, that works out to about three to four days' work plus another day assembling the contraption. While this is still an awful lot of work, it is doubtlessly less than the stone fences. By comparison, with metal posts, clips and barbed wire, I can fence this same area in four hours. Barbed wire wins out east. And in the many parts of the Great Plains, where wood and rocks were in a short supply, barbed wire was the only option.

Worm fences and stone fences were the rule in the mountains before barb wire. When the state had nearly no people, the old-timers literally let the livestock have the run of the hills. No fences needed. Hogs fed on acorns, chestnuts, and whatever else they could find. These animals often saw the farmstead only a couple of weeks before slaughter. They were usually rounded up, fed on corn or scraps for a few weeks, and then killed for winter meat. Even in these parts of the state, animals such as dairy cows were usually kept near the house. This required some kind of fencing. As the population of the state grew, the farmers kept livestock in fenced fields. Stone fences still ring many of these fields in the eastern panhandle of West Virginia. And these fences will probably be visible 1,000 years from now, barring intentional deconstruction by humans.

Worm fences were more common in the mountains. Chestnut and oak were preferred species for the fences. They split well and resisted rot. Many chestnut fences split before, or shortly after chestnut blight hit in the early 1900's, are still standing, fencing pastures long overgrown by trees.

While these fences are an intergenerational asset, the world changes pretty quickly. A fenced three acre pasture may have been an indispensable asset for a family with a dairy cow. Now many of these assets are growing moss.

Ancient Roses and Rhubarb

The mountains were the last places in the east to jump into the modern world. Even now, with interstate highways, it is hard to get into and out of much of the state. The availability of produce not locally grown, such as strawberries and watermelon in winter, is still a real novelty in many small mountain towns. Most families had raised large vegetable gardens and had a patch of flowers. As the mountains began to depopulate and many of the residents moved into town or went to adjacent states to look for work, these gardens became overgrown. Often, the houses deteriorated and rotted away leaving only a few signs of this mountain horticulture: ancient roses and rhubarb.

I think rhubarb can nearly last forever. About four years ago, a neighbor decided they didn't want the seventy-year-old rhubarb that grew by their driveway. They had mowed it off for many years, but it kept coming back up. With all the rhubarb that I had planted in my yard, they figured that I might want an extra one. Of course I would, I told them and went over straight away to dig it up.

I started by digging a circle around the rhubarb and found that this plant had an enormous taproot. This root was over a foot thick. As I dug, the root kept going deeper. I dug down three feet, about as far as I could go without digging up their garage or the adjacent road. No signs of this root getting smaller. So, I had the idea of prying the plant out of the ground. After I broke that shovel, I went back to the house and got a tilling spade (a skinny shovel used for digging really deep, skinny trenches). At about five feet down, the root showed no sign of getting smaller. I used the spade to cut through the root and pry the plant out. This in itself this was surprisingly difficult. I could not carry this monstrosity, so I threw it on a cart and hauled it over to my place. I planted it in what looked like a shallow grave in my yard. I refilled the grave I dug on the neighbor's property with my leftover soil and a bunch of compost. The next spring, the scraps of the leftover roots from four feet down, sprouted by my neighbor's garage. Needless to say, rhubarb is an amazing plant.

Rhubarb must have been a pretty common food in the mountains. Most old farmsteads have a few remaining plants. They are common enough that it is an oddity NOT to find them after a place has been abandoned.

Ancient roses are a bit less common than rhubarb, but I have seen them in some remarkable places. In one of the state forests, not too far over the border in Pennsylvania, a small pink rose managed to hang around after being abandoned many years ago. About twenty feet from the state forest road, this little rose survived, despite overgrowth by both trees and grass and heavy browsing by deer. If this rose had not been by the road, giving it quite a bit more light than if under a full forest canopy, it wouldn't have survived this long. It continued to live. I have thought about this little rose dozens of times since I left the mountains. It is a real fixture in my memory and I often wonder if it's still there.

The family of my wife's grandfather brought a rose with them from Wales when they immigrated to the United States a LONG time ago. Her ancestors must have greatly valued this rose to have carried across the ocean as one of their few possessions. Because this plant root suckered intensely, family members that wanted a part of "granddad's rose" simply took a root sucker and grew it out. One of the last of these root suckers resided at my mother-in-law's house. As my mother-in-law aged, she sold her house to ease some of the maintenance burden that she faced with a fixed income. We dug up the little rose and gave it to my step-daughter. She planted him on her family's land and I hope he is okay. The place where the little rose had grown on my mother-in-law's property sprouted more of granddad's roses until an apartment building went up on top of him. Progress can be harsh.

Surprisingly, I can barely remember anything about granddad's rose. Memory is a strange thing. The rose on the side of a state forest road, with no real connection to my family has been a real fixture in my memory. I think about him whenever I see an old rose struggling. But granddad's rose, rich with family history, I haven't thought about for several years. I have moved so many times in the last twenty years, and left so many people and things behind, that one rose is really pretty minor. But, in thinking about the little rose, I miss the family connection. I plan to call and ask my step-daughter how granddad's rose is and see if she can send me a root sucker. If it came over from Wales on a month-long boat trip and survived…a trip through the US Postal Service should be a rather minor obstacle. I think my wife will really appreciate seeing him.

The house I owned in Staples, Minnesota, had a little Scotchbrier Rose. The little fellow root suckered powerfully, not unlike granddad's rose. He only bloomed once a year, but when he did, creamy white blooms covered him. I transplanted these little root suckers all over the yard. He did well in the sun and the shade, the tough little guy. I knew I would miss him when I moved. I transplanted a couple of little root suckers, packed them up, and carted them to my new home in the Oak Openings of Wisconsin. He now resides next to the 100 year old hen house. He is starting to sucker powerfully again and I plan to make a dozen more little Scotchbriers, a connection to my life in Minnesota.

Beans and Cornbread

The young leave the mountains,
There is nothing there for them,
The future is at a distance,
And they have to travel to live their dreams.

The young leave the mountains,
They travel far from the shadows of the hills,
From the sounds of water rushing over rocks,
From the sounds of winds rushing down the hollows,
From the taste of the beans and cornbread.

The young leave the mountains,
But the ground never looks right,
Without the long dark shadows,
That the mountains cast for most of the day.

The young leave the mountains,
But the water never looks right,
Flowing over sand and mud streambeds,
On its lazy course to the sea.

The young leave the mountains,
But nightfall never feels right,
Without the sound of the wind blowing down
the hollows,
As the sky grows dark and the lightening bugs start
to fly.

The young leave the mountains,
And they spend the rest of their lives craving beans

and cornbread,
Because beans and cornbread taste like the shadows of
the mountains,
And like the rushing mountain streams, and the wind
blowing down the hollows.

And everyone in the mountains says,
They'll come back for the beans and cornbread.

West Virginia's most valued economic export is
its youth. I am one of them. The combined economic power of this loss far exceeds any other industrial
or natural resource product that the state could ever
conceive of selling. My experience with leaving the
mountains has not been that different from the others
who left before me. There are not many jobs in West
Virginia and even fewer for people with specialized
skills. Most leave, but everyone that stays says, "They'll
be back for beans and cornbread."

If West Virginia had a state dish, beans and
cornbread would be it. Probably for over one thousand years, beans and cornbread have been a staple of
people living in West Virginia. This may seem an exces-
sively long time for those that consider North American
history to begin with Columbus; however, Native
Americans started planting the "three sisters" of beans,
corn and squash at least 1000 years ago in the Mid-
Atlantic states. Cakes of corn roasted in the coals and
soups of beans and squash are documented through
anthropological and archeological evidence, cultural
writings of early European visitors, and oral tradi-
tions of tribes and bands. As neither beans nor corn
were native to Europe, the early settlers of the moun-

tains learned to grow these crops from the Native Americans. Many of the fields of the early European settlers were planted on old fields cleared by the Native Americans. This tradition of food has continued basically unbroken (although with a few refinements) for over 1000 years. Saying that beans and cornbread are indigenous to the area is quite accurate. These foods really are part of the unique flavor of the mountains.

Growing up in the mountains means you eat beans OFTEN. Many of the older people in the area have their own special beans obtained from family members that they have grown their whole life. Red coats, corn field beans, bird egg beans, yellow eye beans, and white half-runners are only a few of the many old-style beans that you can still occasionally find. Most people now buy store-bought beans. At less than 50 cents a pound, it is hard to justify growing, drying and shelling out beans. However, the store provides little selection, offering pintos (most people call them brown beans), and navy or great northern beans (called white beans).

Each of the old beans has its own place. There are two kinds of beans: bush beans and pole beans. Bush beans grow like bushes rather than vines. They set nearly all of their beans at once and then die in a process called determinate fruiting. So bush beans are good for things like canning, where you need a lot of beans at once. Pole beans on the other hand, produce their beans continuously and grow like vines. These beans are better when you need a small amount all season long to supply your dinner every couple of days. Half-runners are the exception to these rules and answer the question about which type of plant should be used. Half-runners begin to grow like bush beans with determinant fruiting. They make a good size batch of beans at one time, so that someone could can or freeze a winter's supply on time. After this, half-runners send out indeterminate fruiting shoots which supply small amounts of beans for the rest of the summer, making them the perfect bean.

Cornfield beans are another "perfect" bean. They are a type of pinto selected to grow under corn (sort of a modern version of the "three sisters" plantings). Bean roots grow a special type of nodule that supplies the home for rhizobium (a tiny microbe). These rhizobium take nitrogen out of the air (where it is not available for plants) and fix it in a form that is usable to plants. Beans tend to have moderate nitrogen needs; however, corn has a massive need for this specific nutrient. Cornfield beans supply this nitrogen (at least a part of it) to the corn plant. In turn, the beans get the corn stalks to climb on. This makes a good match. Cornfield beans tend to breakdown while cooking. If you use them as only part of the beans in a recipe, they cook down into a thick rich soup.

Another type is yellow-eye beans. I have never seen yellow-eye beans in any store. I have seen them for sale at a couple of farmer's markets and in one seed catalog. Yellow-eye taste and grow more like cowpeas than beans. They are very drought tolerant and high yielding. They sound perfect, but some people just don't like them (including me). Yellow-eye beans taste like grass.

Beans are usually cooked as soup, regardless of the type. A chunk of ham bone or hock, some onion, maybe some cracklings (the crispy fried out pork fat that is left over from rendering lard), and a carrot are all that is needed. The beans are soaked overnight, cooked slowly all day, and eaten in the evening with cornbread.

The cornbread itself varies so much it is sometimes hard to call it by the same name. Some people make a sweet cornbread that is fluffy and moist like a cake. Other people make a cornbread that is so dense and dry that you have to shave it off with a knife to soak in the soup. Some people bake the cornbread. Others cook it like a fat tortilla on the stove or make it like pancakes. However one makes it, the bread is to be eaten in the soup, either crumbled on top or split in half with beans poured over it. That's a meal

Having been through much of the U.S., I can tell you that most people just don't eat beans very often (except in the Southwest, Tex-Mex foods). Those that do eat beans think of them as a poor substitute for food. They do it out of desperation or as a way to save money. In the mountains, beans and cornbread are a part of the culture. You miss them like a relative you haven't seen for a while. They are a comfort food.

For many of those that leave the mountains to chase their dreams or make a living, the rest of the world never feels like home. Beans and cornbread dull the homesickness a bit.

My mountains were full of riches that left while poor people that stayed. The hills and hollows are naturally endowed with geological riches: coal, oil, gas, metallic ores, and salt. The thin layer of soil that covers most of these minerals supports an impressive biological wealth of timber, botanicals, foods and game. With a little help, this soil can grow crops and livestock. The water that flows from this soil supports a cold water fishery of brook trout and warm water fisheries of pan fish, bass and catfish.

With resources like this, my mountains were literally a Garden of Eden: a garden that could have been managed for the wealth and happiness of its people. Instead, it was plundered by wealthy "outsiders" who cared nothing about the place and left when the riches were exhausted. This legacy of destruction still haunts my mountains.

COAL

A couple of months ago, I made a Mother's Day slideshow for my mother that included photos from her youth set to the music of my kids and I singing Loretta Lynn's "Coal Miner's Daughter." My mother was a coal miner's daughter in a family of Italian and Spanish immigrants who had to scratch pretty hard to make ends meet. Being raised a "coal miner's daughter" shapes one's identity: an identity of hard work and a rural lifestyle. This identity fits with the mountains.

The United States has HALF A TRILLION tons of minable coal. My mountains have a demonstrated coal reserve of 36 billion tons, according to the Office of Surface Mining Regulation and Enforcement. In the little county of Boone, where I grew up, more than 80 percent of the entire surface of the county was minable: the largest concentration of coal per square mile anywhere in the world. To say the least, the history of coal intertwines with that of my mountains.

A little stream called Pond Fork flows near the house I lived in as a kid. The Pond Fork flows into the Little Coal River which then flows into the Coal River. This river was the stage of one of the biggest discoveries in West Virginia history. In the mid 1700s, John Peter Salley took a trip through central West Virginia and discovered the first natural outcrops of coal along a river that he named Coal River, which runs not all that far downstream from my house. The land was extremely inaccessible, but huge quantities of money could be made from that coal if it could be transported to urban and industrial markets. In less than 100 years, the state started to mine. Early miners used tools that were not that different from what was used in their gardens, tools like shovels and picks. However, with the influx of external money and expertise, the coal fields began to expand. Most importantly for the future of the state, the mineral rights (and in some cases land), were sold to outside investors because the people in the mountains had no clue of the value of coal. This escalated the scale of the impact economically, culturally, and environmentally.

It is hardly possible to overemphasize the impact of coal on the social fabric of West Virginia or, for that matter, my family. Both of my grandfathers mined (one in West Virginia and one in Pennsylvania). Both breathed in coal dust for years. Both spent years "laid off" from the mines and scrounged a living running various businesses. Both developed black lung (a disease where coal dust becomes imbedded in the lungs and reduces lung capacity), and both died carrying a part of the mine in their lungs with them to the grave.

In recent years, deaths in the mines have gone down due to more stringent regulations and increased mechanization. While deaths after years of mining due to black lung, silicosis (another rock dust originating lung ailment), and other work-related diseases are a chronic reminder of years of hard work, deaths due to mine catastrophes pose another serious risk. The largest mine disaster on record anywhere in the world happened in West Virginia. Over three hundred people died in one mine in the early 1900s. Even today in 2006, West Virginia has been faced with a mine disaster and two separate mining deaths in one week, prompting the governor to shut down all mining operations for "safety inspections." Mining is safer now, but not risk-free.

This past history of poor mine safety conditions and poor business practices prompted one of the most eventful unionization efforts in the history of this country. To understand the effect of unions in the state, a person really needs to re-adjust the version of history taught in most textbooks. History textbooks forget the places where natural resources are extracted. They forget the people who actually mined or harvested the resources. And they usually forget the turmoil that is left afterwards. Most times, they only mention the consequences for a few rich people living in some big city who exercise their will on innumerable poor people. Essentially, these textbooks forget West Virginia.

West Virginia was an inaccessible backwater in an otherwise booming United States' economy. The hills and hollows acted as an incubator for some of the most independent people in the world - people who had survived off what they could grow, harvest, or barter for many generations; people that lived in clan societies and for who the clan was the family unit. West Virginia was a collection of clans and communities but not really a state. It was a state created out of resentment towards the "rich people" living in tidewater Virginia who did not care about "ignorant" mountain people. Mountain people do not like to have things dictated to them. They knew the taste of freedom and resented the Virginian government for creating laws, regulations and taxes that the mountain people felt did not benefit them.

With the advent of coal came phenomenal social changes. People moved out of the "hollows" and into the coal towns. People that had never worked for "wages," whose lives were based on working independently and bartering, became "employees" and "consumers." They became dependent on the same support system of grocery stores and factories that defined the rest of the country at that point in history. Even greater changes occurred, as new immigrants from Europe arrived to work the mines.

With these coal towns came goods from outside of the mountains, and suddenly items that people had never had became available. Concepts like "debt" became realities. Often, miners had to work several months just to break even from buying their tools. Working conditions were usually abysmal. Pay was low and in company "script" (coupons made by the coal company that equated to money).

Workers bought all personal items from the company store with this script. The company store set the prices and chose what items to carry. Miners lived in company housing which was basically mass produced houses of the same design.

Almost every aspect of the miners' lives was controlled by the company: their jobs, houses, food, clothing, and even their churches. With such tight control of people's lives, abuses were all too likely. While some companies operated fairly, many would cheat the miners. Cribbing (paying the miners for each "one ton" coal car mined even though the coal cars held more than one ton) was common, as was docking for slate in the coal. The safety issues, the inability to control debt, the general lack of control of personal life, and the constant cheating by the companies set conditions for revolt. It also set the stage for the United Mine Workers of America (UMWA).

Let's skip ahead a bit in history now. Skip the blood and tears of the mine wars, the intimidation and murders by employees of the Baldwin-Felts Detective Agency, the murders committed by the miners, the strikes and tent cities, and the desperation of watching wives and children evicted from company housing. Skip characters that are only known to West Virginian's, like Mother Jones and Sid Hatfield. It is human nature to always talk about wars and skip the peaceful periods between. I am going to turn that on its head. The story of unionization is a story of the results, not a story of war. The involvement of unions increased the rights of the individual miners, their level of pay rose to more fairly compensate the risks taken every day, and also improved the level of overall mine safety. The ideal union is powerful enough to erase the need for strikes. Unionization changed the face of mining.

Mining has changed dramatically over the years. While huge labor forces and basic tools fueled the mining industry in the late 1800s, today huge equipment and minimal labor forces keep the industry going. The mining industry employs a total of 40,000 people according to the West Virginia Office of Miners' Health, Safety, and Training. This includes everyone, not just the actual miners. Employment by the mining industry declines annually. With this decline goes one of the few adequate paying jobs in these communities.

West Virginia has two kinds of mines: deep mines and surface mines. Deep mines use various types of boring and tunneling technology to remove coal with minimal disturbance of the ground surface. Many ancient deep mines are so inconspicuous that they pose a danger to hikers and hunters walking in the forests. Surface mines are not so inconspicuous.

Surface mines remove the overburden (the soil and rock covering the coal seam), remove the coal, and then replace the overburden. The site is then "reclaimed" to a semi-natural condition. While many old, abandoned "strip mines" (the colloquial name for surface mines) still scar the landscape, the majority of mines since The Surface Mining Control and Reclamation Act of 1977, have been or will be reclaimed. While the landscape is altered, the impacts of the mining are less drastic than the old strip mines. This also reduces the risk of acid mine drainage.

Besides the altered landscapes, another problem that occurs is acid mine drainage. Acid mine drainage is an insidious problem in my mountains. The broken rock and often the coal itself contains compounds like iron pyrites that upon exposure to water, oxygen and some bacteria creates an acidic brew. This brew contains whatever metals are in the rocks and can include iron, manganese, zinc, aluminum and even in at least one case, gold. This toxic brew proceeds to the nearest waterway and kills it. Many of West Virginia's streams are orange because of the precipitated iron from the acid mine drainage and are essentially dead.

All of this creates the ambivalent feeling that mountain people have toward coal. Mountain people know hard work; many of them wear it like a badge and are proud of it. They are proud of the mining that their parents or grandparents did to fuel the growth of the country. They are proud of how their grandparents scraped by on nothing. They talk with pride that the largest dragline in the world operated just on the other side of the mountain. These things are part of what built their world. But they also hate the damage from the past. These mountain people live with the poisoned rivers from the old scars and orange-stained clothing from running iron tainted "sulfur water" through their washing machines. They live with mountaintop removal mines that scrape the tops off of mountains to get at the coal and then dump this overburden into the adjacent "hollows." They live with the scars of these past mines but very little of the pesky money these mines generate. That money is controlled by other people living a different life in a distant place: outsiders.

The old wounds left by poor business practices of mine operators from 100 years ago still fester, even if they are removed by four or five generations. These old wounds have left a fear of "outsiders" in the mountains. Being born a "coal miner's daughter" (to quote the songs), like my mother, comes with an acceptance of the inevitable needs of a prosperous country for energy and the needs of a family for a solid income. It also comes with the taint of regret for all the past years of loss to black lung and roof falls, loss to the mountains from acid mine drainage and old mine scars, and loss to the future because of the economic desolation left in many mountain towns.

LOGGING

In the late 1800's, the country was industrializing and building. This growth fed off of a wealth of natural resources. The same force that spawned the immense growth of the coal industry also spurred the timber industry along. Homes and businesses needed to be built as towns and cities were expanded. The "hordes of Europe" crossed over to the "land of opportunity." All of this required resources like wood and coal.

During the late 1800s and even into today, more timber was used in building than nearly any other resource. Railroads absorbed millions of ties to build rail lines. Mines absorbed even more for roof timbers and props. Fencing (before barbed wire), posts, barns and wagons, were needed for all the farms.

Timber from the mountains provided the largest portion of what built the factories, towns, rail lines, and farms that made industrialization and urban living possible. Timber and coal helped feed a boom happening across the United States; a boom whose economic development is still easily seen in states like Maryland, Virginia, eastern New York, and Pennsylvania. This doesn't even include long-gone infrastructure like bridges, or extractives like tannin from tree bark (used to tan hides). Even the humble clothespin was made from beech trees cut in the mountains. This boom benefited large parts of the East Coast; however, it left few benefits in the mountains and many scars.

Between the late 1800s and 1920, nearly all of the timber in the entire state of West Virginia was logged. More than 75% of the state was originally forested. Cutting this enormous forest proved an immense undertaking. Trees as large as 13 feet in diameter were cut by hand. With the help of horses, mules, and specially designed logging engines (Shay engines), the entire state was logged. During many years the rate of logging was over one billion board feet a year - a feat nearly impossible to comprehend. And, as with most stories of natural resource extraction played out across the world, the money went elsewhere, leaving the area of extraction impoverished, at least for a while. The difference with this resource is that, while the old timbers were "mined" unsustainably out of the forest, the land began to re-vegetate. Thanks to the rejuvenating power of the mountain forests, the land healed.

In the year 2006, more than 80 years after the end of the heaviest wave of logging, the original forestland of the state is nearly totally reforested. While the giants are mostly gone, timber harvest is still one of the top five industries in the state. This timber harvest is not "timber mining" and it is much more sustainable. I will not pretend that timber harvesting is at the level of sustainability that it needs to be for the long-term benefit of the forest and the people, but it is better than the whole-scale slaughter at the turn of the century. We still have "high-grading," which is cutting the best and leaving the rest. "The rest" are usually poor quality trees that will never be of timber quality or often even of wildlife value. This kind of harvest is a debt against the future but it is recoverable. This forest is a "renewable resource" that has the chance to re-grow and be cut again...on many sites, this could be continued forever.

THE DIFFERENCE BETWEEN COAL AND TIMBER

Mining coal and harvesting timber are dominant industries in the mountains. Both can be utilized in a thoughtful manner that will limit damage. The real difference between timber and coal is that once coal is gone, it's gone. Ask any retired miner living next to an abandoned mine. They may re-open a mine and haul out another lower seam, but basing a lifestyle on a non-renewable resource is precarious at best. Basing a lifestyle on a renewable resource can be an investment in the future. Good timber management leaves the stands better than when the loggers entered them. Careful harvest leaves hope for the future. Long after the coal is gone, if the mountains are still there (which may be in question with some types of mining), the timber will grow.

This timber will leave jobs and resources for the descendants of the turn-of-the-century loggers... and for the descendents of the coal miners.

Leaving the Mountains

If it wasn't for the mountains, I wonder if the populations of Ohio and Michigan might just dry up. On the main arteries heading out of the mountains, Interstates 79, 64, and 77, you will see loaded down cars and old pickups heading off to new lives. Michigan and Ohio catch most of the refugees from the economic hardships of the mountains. Back home, there are only so many jobs for miners and loggers and only so many jobs in body shops or as mechanics. These are about the only good paying jobs that many towns have to offer. College graduates are even less likely to stay in the mountains. How many mechanical engineers, school teachers or biologists can a small mountain town use? If my experience with my job searches is correct, the percentage employed in the mountains is a slight bit higher than zero and I apparently was not meant to be one of them. Ultimately, the lack of professional jobs sends yet another refugee off on the Hillbilly Highway.

My whole family, for generations, has been economic refugees. My grandparents were economic refugees from Europe. My maternal grandmother's family emigrated from Spain. My maternal grandfather's family emigrated from Italy. The story's the same on my father's side, albeit with different countries inserted, although I know somewhat less about them. My father and mother were economic refugees from West Virginia, for a while. They worked in Maryland, another large refugee camp for West Virginians, where I was born. Like many others, my parents returned to the state to raise their kids. Not many of the refugees want their children to develop "big city ways." Some have no choice, others make some pretty big sacrifices to take their kids "back home." My parents raised me in West Virginia in the hills and hollows until I was a teen. By then, I was already a hillbilly. Now, approaching middle-age, I have yet to develop the feared big city ways.

I attended college. Education is basically the fastest liberator for most of the refugees. My liberation took a bit longer. I kept going to college until I ran out of degrees to get. Got 'em all. Up until my grandmother died, she thought it peculiar that someone could spend so much time in school. I know she was proud of my education, but I also knew that she never really understood parts of it.

Before she died, I'd thankfully made it out of school and was working for a reasonable wage. Even then, though, she never quite understood why my job didn't consist of simply using my brain. My field of expertise, Natural Resources (specifically forestry), is very field-oriented and requires quite a bit of physical effort. She'd always assumed if you went to college, you got a job where you talked and wrote a lot and did not do any "real work" from then on. I expect that my tales of covering 13 miles of woods in a day, carrying 60 pound backpacks, conducting tree planting projects, and working in 10 below weather, confused the heck out of her. Why did I need to be "doing work like that", I went to college? And while she was at it, "when was I moving back to West Virginia?" "Was I really going to raise my kids out in the flatlands where it was so cold?" I was working in the Midwest when she died. I don't ever plan to leave.

From these little anecdotes, you can tell that I love the mountains. I will die a hillbilly, but not in the hills. I won't forget the sound of water rushing over rocks or the taste of wild trout cooked in butter or the smell of a whole mountaintop of sourwood in bloom or the feeling of a thunderstorm echoing off the mountains. I miss it some days.

But as much as my mountains are beautiful, they are really hard to live in. Few jobs exist for me (and remember I am in natural resources, something in which the state is rich) and even fewer for my kids. My son is a mechanical genius with a curious mind. He grabs a piece of information from here, one from there, and makes a knowledge sandwich. I know very few adults that can think "outside the box" like my son. He is only 11. I have never seen anyone with the gifts that he has. I do not want him to have to beg an autoshop to let him fix cars because working in the local convenience store or on the grade line at the sawmill are his only available options.

My daughter is skilled with animals and has an artist's eye. When she sits in my sheep pasture, my sheep approach her like she is one of the flock. She knows which ones don't feel well and can tell me which ones I need to check for something. She will grab a sheep or a hen or jump in the hog pen with no fear. She is observant, empathetic and fearless...a pure soul. What can she do with these gifts in the mountains? Maybe work as a telemarketer at one of the new companies that have set up shop next to the cheap labor. But no one should have to work for less than $6 an hour. Not too many years ago my wife, my oldest, and I were living off a similarly Spartan-like income. If the country won't boost the minimum wage, as it hasn't for some time, I want to keep my kids away from where that is all they will get paid.

And then one must worry about the violence. My mountains have always been a bit volatile. Clan wars and coal wars may be the only thing that outsiders know about West Virginia. Hatfield's and McCoy's: we had the former clan, Kentucky had the latter. In recent years, the advent of television has not done much to quell violence and depression. TV shows the people in West Virginia everything that they don't have.

For the first three grades, I went to a small school with about 100 kids in grades 1-6. The school was so small, that there were two grade levels to a room. There were an awful lot of fights for such a tiny school. A lot of these fights were based on things that relatives of one student had done to relatives of the other student. They were not fighting each other as much as they were fighting each other's families.

This is one way the Upper Midwest differs from West Virginia. I have asked my children about the fights in school. There apparently aren't any…at all…ever. I have not heard of any fights in the five years my son has been in school. I got in fights at least once every year that I was in school in the mountains. I was a very mild child; never started a fight, only finished them. Most of the fights that I was in were basically attacks. These attacks were usually based on things that my parents (school teachers) did to someone's brother or sister. I love that my kids do not have to worry about being beat up when they go to school…or even worse, being proud that they beat someone up. The Midwest does not approach to the world this way.

Besides the jobs and the lack of violence, the Midwest also accepts outsiders. You can move to the other side of the mountain in West Virginia and you will always be an OUTSIDER. You are, after all, from the other side of the mountain. The Midwest has always followed the words of Emma Lazarus' poem about the Statue of Liberty, "Give me your tired, your poor, your huddled masses yearning to breathe free…." Political and economic refuges like the Somalis, Hmong, Vietnamese, Russians and Mexicans have found a quite welcoming home in the Upper Midwest. Many will tell you that this is the best place they have ever lived.

I am an outsider here, and yet I am not treated like one. I have met people out here that treat me like family, and have returned the favor. I have been stuck on the side of the road and picked up several times— never once killed. I have had a guy on a snowmobile stop to let me use a cell phone to call a tow truck for my stuck car. You can leave the doors of your house open and you will find everything when you get back. More than a few times I have found the addition of rhubarb, zucchini, and tomatoes. Sort of a reverse thievery (especially with the zucchini). I never bothered to lock the car; too much chance of locking the keys in. In winter, you can actually go to the stores around here and find unlocked cars sitting in parking lots running because it's too cold to turn them off and there's little chance of them getting stolen. I leave things like tools, rolls of wire, fishing rods, you name it, sitting out at my farm that I would never consider leaving out when I lived in West Virginia. I have had friends in the mountains with cheap things like rolls of baling wire and bales of straw stolen, for who knows why. This usually doesn't happen out here. Even the teenage boys, who in the mountains often can be jerks, show respect in the Midwest. It took my wife over a year to lose her apprehension about walking by a group of teenagers. Teenagers here say thank you and hold doors. If you go to a packed meeting and you look really tired or you are old, often people will offer you their seat. You have to accept it. To reject it is to reject their kindness. And surrounded by this, it is hard not to act that way yourself. And it makes you feel good. There exists hardly a more welcoming place to move than the Midwest, and I do not plan on leaving.

Moving to
    the Oak Openings
        and Prairies

Lutefisk, Lefse, Friday Fish Fries, Brats and Cheese Curds

I love living in the Upper Midwest: the land of lutefisk and lefse. As a Minnesotan, I lived in a little town called Staples, the lutefisk epicurean center of the world.

For the uninitiated, lutefisk is a specially prepared fish dish characteristic of Scandinavian countries. As much of the population of northern Minnesota is at least partly Scandinavian (or at least fakes it, so as not to be ostracized), they serve this dish at special occasions to connect to their culture. For most people, lutefisk is a difficult meal to eat.

First, there is the smell. Lutefisk is cod that is air dried on racks until it hardens enough to pound in nails. This is not an exaggeration as lutefisk aficionados demonstrate it regularly as a joke. If they stopped at this stage, it would be no different than the Spanish baccala. But the Scandinavians have a special way to prepare the salt cod. The fish soaks in several changes of water over the course of a week. It then soaks in a solution of either birch ashes and water (a mild natural lye solution) or a commercial solution of lye for a week. After this soaking, it once again gets soaked in several changes of water to remove the poisonous effects of the lye. At this point the lutefisk is ready to cook.

As you would expect, this process does not smell particularly sweet. Even after the fish has been soaked repeatedly, a process that one would think would eliminate most of the smell and taste, good or bad, the lutefisk still has a bit of an odor. Places such as churches that have annual lutefisk dinners do not cook the lutefisk inside. The smell wouldn't leave indoors, so they usually cook it outside. The advent of outdoor turkey cookers have made this process nearly too easy. This already heavily processed food can be either boiled or baked, and this makes any true Scandinavian feel at home.

I have not yet acquired a taste for this fish. I have tried it and found it to taste soapy and have a gelatinous texture. The soapy taste derives from the reaction with the lye in a process not too dissimilar from the preparation of old-style lye soap. The gelatinous texture is surely due to the length of processing required for the product. Most Scandinavians that I have talked to about lutefisk insist that I have simply eaten poorly done lutefisk. They may be right; however, I am still withholding judgment.

It is impossible to speak of lutefisk without mentioning lefse. While lutefisk lacks the curb appeal of…well…basically anything else, lefse is a widely acceptable food. I have yet to meet anyone that did not like it (except maybe a few people on diets). Lefse is basically a tortilla made out of potatoes and flour. I first tried lefse at a maple producers meeting. Lefse with maple sugar and butter may be the best dessert of all time: basic, fresh and so good.

Like lutefisk, making lefse is basic but not easy. Boiled potatoes are run though a potato ricer. The potato ricer, basically a hand-operated kitchen tool used to squeeze potatoes through little tiny holes in metal, mashes them. Modern cooks use rehydrated instant mashed potatoes. Flour and cream (or milk) is added before the dough is gently kneaded and allowed to rest. After it rests, it gets rolled out on a floured towel using an extra heavy rolling pin (more of a club actually). Using a special wooden spatula called a lefse stick (made specifically for this purpose), the flattened lefse is raised up from the towel and cooked on a lefse griddle. Believe it or not, most hardware stores in central Minnesota sell these griddles, shallow electric fry pans that get ridiculously hot. The lefse are flipped only once using the lefse stick and then removed from the pan.

The first time I ate these lefse, I loved them. I mean, I really loved them. I begged poor Mrs. Kroll to show me how to make them. In a couple of minutes I was turning them out perfectly; however, I lost my touch when I tried them the next night at home. They tasted delicious but were thicker and ugly. It took me about a dozen times on my own to get them right. The dough has to rest. The potatoes must be completely squished. Only russet potatoes work. You have to really work the flour into the towels. The rolling pin has to be enormous. You have to have a lefse stick to flip them. Nothing else works. However, after you have got it figured out, the process works well. Lefse just might be the perfect food: definitely something to serve with lutefisk. Sort of a yin and yang, good versus evil thing.

If you do not like the idea of lutefisk and lefse, there is still the Friday fish fry. Nearly every bar and restaurant has an all-you-can eat Friday fish fry. Remember now, in northern Minnesota, we are talking about farmers or loggers, or at least the grown kids of farmers and loggers. They see all-you-can eat as a challenge and most are quite amazing contenders. Coming from a family that views all-you-can eat as a sport, I felt right at home.

The Friday fish fry is nearly always comprised of the same menu. A generic, usually unrecognizable fish, (cod, Pollock, whiting, etc.) breaded in crumbs and flour, then deep-fried until crispy. Add either a baked potato or fries and coleslaw and you have the full meal. It is simple, delicious, and a comfort food if eaten in good company with happy people.

When I moved to Wisconsin, they still had the Friday fish fry; however, they added another meal: the brat fry/boil. Delicious, greasy spiced sausages are boiled in beer until fully cooked. Then these cooked brats are either pan fried or grilled. Some people grill them straight, but that eliminates the flavor of the beer and adds to the chance of explosion. Brats cooked raw will inevitably have one exploder. No matter how many holes you poke in the buggers to let out the hot grease, it will no doubt build up and BANG: brat shrapnel. So the risk-averse people that like the flavor of beer…read this to mean people from Wisconsin…boil the brats first.

And last, but not least, the humble cheese curd. A cheese curd, for the uninitiated, is an intermediate step in the cheddar making process. The cheese is prepared and then cut; however, instead of packing, pressing and aging, they are eaten fresh. Really fresh… "so fresh that they squeak" according to a local radio advertisement for a local brand. And trust me, they squeak. I had eaten cheese curds before in both Pennsylvania and Minnesota that consisted of small chunks of cheddar. Little did I know, until I moved to Wisconsin, that I'd been served old, inferior curds.

I bought my first batch on our way to look at a farm we hoped to buy in Wisconsin. I love to eat locally and support local businesses, so I stopped at a cheese factory with a retail store. They had a dozen varieties of cheese and all were delicious. I bought some for my wife and me. I never even considered tasting the curds because I thought I knew them well. I bought a bag for the kids along with some cured sausages (beer sticks to the locals) for the rest of the drive.

The kids were overjoyed at the prospect of eating cured meat and cheese (two of their favorite foods). We opened the bag and they started eating. Then I heard a squeaking like a mouse coming from the back seat. I asked them what was making the noise. They replied, "the cheese curds." I tried one. They really are squeaky little buggers. Sort of disconcerting. I have eaten well over a hundred types of cheese made all over this country and all over the world. I had NEVER had cheese that squeaks. Within the next 10 or 15 miles, the radio ad came on that said "so fresh that they squeak" and we all laughed. We were moving to a new life yet again but I knew that I would love it here. How can you help but love a state with cheese shops every 30 miles or so (on the main roads) where gorgonzola is sold along side of squeakin' cheese curds. Something about it just screams HOME.

Wild Rice

The canoe being pushed through the water
By the arms of a standing man,
Another in the front of the canoe,
Two flail sticks gently combing the rice grains into the
canoe.

The mild sulfur smell of the water,
Muskrats gliding by the boat,
The heat of the sun
A cloud of mosquitoes.

The canoe slides among the aquatic prairie
Grains of rice with hulls and long awns build up
As do thousands of "rice worms" and beetles
At the hands of a gentle, human threshing machine.

The rice must be dried at the end of the day
And then parched to open the hulls
Gently worked to free the hulls
And winnowed to blow away the chaff.

The spirit of the rice comes from the water
The flails, the wood smoke and the heat,
The flavor from the care to make sure
That nowhere is it cheated.

Before I moved to the open savannas of
central Wisconsin and even before I lived on the
prairie in central Minnesota, I did not know much
about wild rice. I had eaten it before and had even

seen the plants on a few lakes, but that was about it. After I moved to Minnesota, I learned about the miracle God made when he created wild rice.

Oral history of the Anishinaabe says that they came to the place where food grew on the water. They came looking for the Mahnomen, literally translated to "the god's gift of grain." And it was.

Wild rice is a type of grass that grows in slowly moving water in the Lake States and central Canada. The grass grows from the mud in the bottom of the rice beds from two to six feet under water. The rice ripens indeterminately (only part of the head at a time) allowing each rice bed to be harvested three or more times. It pays to be very gentle with the rice heads, because you may see them many times.

To harvest a rice bed, a canoe is pushed through the bed with a long pole. The pole has a metal contraption on the bottom called a duck foot, which prevents the pole from sinking too far into the mud. The person pushes this pole while standing in the canoe for maximum mechanical advantage. Several hours of this are a real day's work. Someone else sits in the front of the boat and uses two ricing sticks, sometimes called flails, to gently knock the grains off of the heads. With one stick, the ricer leans the heads over the boat. With the other stick, the ricer taps the heads. This gentle tapping is all that is needed to dislodge the ripe seeds. Unripe seeds do not finish well, so there is no reason to harvest them. If the plant is treated roughly, the harvester will not be able to harvest the rest of the seeds when they are ripe. Despite its name, flailing rice is a very careful, gentle process, which forces those with rough tendencies to slow down and use caution.

Finishing the rice is another issue entirely. To produce the best rice, everything needs to be done very quickly. Those that want to make light colored, mild flavored rice dry the rice immediately. As soon as possible, the feed bags full of rice are opened and spread out to start the drying process. After the rice has begun to dry, it might be transferred to racks in order to speed the process, or it might just be periodically turned. In the next step, known as parching, the rice is roasted in any of a number of ways. Many people use a metal drum rotated over a wood fire, while others use large metal sheets. I have even seen an old car hood placed over a fire and used to parch the rice. But the key element is the application of even heat and some method of constant stirring.

After the rice is lightly parched, the hulls and awns are more easily removed. The rice can be treaded under foot or gently struck using a traditional mortar and pestle-like piece of equipment. As far as I know, this instrument has no special name. Essentially the pestle is gently struck against the rice, in an effort not to break any of the rice, but hard enough to jostle the grains and separate the hulls. The resulting rice can be winnowed using the traditional method. In this method a pan is used to toss the rice into the air and to catch it as it falls while the chaff blows away in the wind. This is a skill that requires much practice. A modern device called an air machine can also be used. The air machine is basically a fan that directs a stream of air through a stream of falling grains. The grains fall through the air current with no problem. This light chaff is blown away, resulting in clean rice.

During the August/early September harvest, Native Americans moved into ricing camps. They would rice for weeks and celebrate the first harvest, which was considered a great blessing. Freshly harvested rice is the lightest in color and the mildest in flavor. It also cooks very fast. When people talk about this type of rice they say, "It is still a little green." The rice that is finished after having waited for several days is much darker and has a stronger flavor. This rice also takes much longer to cook. Most commercially produced paddy rice (domesticated "wild" rice) is finished in the second way. It is all dark and takes a very long time to cook. Many people prefer the light rice to the dark rice. I definitely prefer mine a little green.

After parching, wild rice can store for years. It is a very compact way to carry calories. It is high in protein, delicious, and nearly a complete food in itself. According to the Wisconsin Department of Natural Resources, rice yield per acre of wetland can be over 500 pounds with 50-75 pounds that can be harvested, an amazing yield considering that this is a wild harvested crop from otherwise unfarmable lands. This yield is achieved with no input (with the possible exception of initial seeding by some tribes on wetlands) except harvest and a limited negative environmental impact. A canoe load of rice might finish down to 50 pounds of food. It would be hard to think of a better system, hence the word Mahnomen: "the god's gift of grain."

67

Icy winters, snow snakes and snirt

The sun is getting lower,
And the nights are crisp,
The hard frosts are coming,
The leaves are already kissed.

The killing cold will come,
And the leaves will fall
And after that the snow
Will cover us all.

And then, the long cold winter,
Will descend on the town
Soon we will all be walking
With our eyes cast down.

The winter is coming,
The time is near,
It'll be a cold one
I fear.

      It is hard to describe the Upper Midwest
without talking about cold and snow. This region
is unbelievably cold and windy: FRIGID. When
talking to old friends or family out in the mountains, I
try to explain the cold, but it is really no use. It is so
cold that it defies explanation. How do you explain
negative 42 degrees Fahrenheit (called forty-two below
by the locals)? The Upper Midwest is the only place
where people qualify the degrees BOTH above and

below zero. If it is ten degrees, they say, "It's ten above." If it's negative ten, it is "ten below."

In order to understand the cold in the Midwest, one must realize that the "horrible blizzard and deadly sub-zero weather" which the idiot newscasters out east talk about when New England gets some tiny little blizzard are very similar to what we refer to as our WARM AND PLEASANT DAYS. It gets quite a lot worse than that out here, but on the other hand, at least we know how to drive in it (most of us at least). Because this seems so difficult for the people out east to understand, I have come up with a few standard factoids to tell you in relation to a particularly cold 42-below day in my prairie home.

How cold is 42 below? Imagine the difference between freezing (32 degrees) and a pretty darn hot day (106 degrees). The difference is 74 degrees, right? Is that a pretty big difference? That is the same difference between freezing and 42 below. Freezing (32 degrees) ain't even considered chilly out here. If the temperature gets UP to freezing in spring, people are wearing shorts and at least a couple of idiots will be wearing bathing suits and sitting in lawn chairs (the result of a disease called cabin fever which we will talk about later).

Even though this little factoid should make sense when I talk to the people out east, it usually doesn't. Therefore a few practical examples are needed, so let's proceed to them.

When it gets this cold, weird things start to happen. The first involves car tires. It gets so cold in winter that the car tires go flat on one side. When air gets cold it contracts. Effectively, the air gets smaller and the air pressure of the tires goes down. This is just like a low tire, right? Go to the gas station and add some air, right? Wrong. Because it is so cold, the rubber in the tires is no longer flexible. The side that was next to the ground STAYS FLAT, even as it is rotating down the road. Kbump…kbump…kbump. If it is really cold, this happens for four or five MILES. Due to friction, the tire eventually warms up, the air expands and you are good to go.

During this same weather, the roads you drive on are covered in ice. You see, the road salt and the calcium chloride that the plow trucks put down do not melt the snow until the days get extremely warm, like ten or twelve degrees above. In some cases, this can be a full month or more of waiting. The plow trucks usually scrape the road down to a bed of ice and apply a mix of sand and salt. Driving on ice sounds dangerous, but interestingly, it isn't. As long as the air temperature stays lower than 15 below, the road never is slick. In order for ice to be slick, the ice has to be warm enough that the friction from the tires can melt a miniscule, unnoticeable amount of water to act as a lubricant between the ice and the tire. At 10 or 15 below, that simply doesn't happen. There is not enough heat from the friction to make it slick. With an ice base on the road, a bit of sand for grip when you need to brake, usually applied only on corners and at stop signs, and all of the potholes filled in with ice, you are good to go.

Engine block heaters are also funny. More than about 10 or 15 below, some cars get a bit testy about starting. Push it down to 35 below or colder and most get a bit of an attitude problem, sort of like a teenager that you try to get up at 4:00 AM to go to Aunt Pearl's house for breakfast. After all, the engine oil is basically the consistency of a Chapstick. The fuel injectors and associated sensors have no clue how much fuel they need to inject and if you have an old car with a carburetor, well, it's better not to talk about that. The batteries have hardly any output and the antifreeze is being tested to its maximum. After the cars warm up they run fine. Boy would it be nice if we could somehow just keep the engine warmer, even just a little warmer, so we can just get it started. Thus the engine block heater was created. Engine block heaters are basically contraptions that heat either the antifreeze or the oil. This keeps the engine at or above freezing, warm enough to start. In northern Minnesota, a lot of people plug in their cars in the evening so that they can keep the engine relatively warm. The only people who plug in their cars out east are those who have electric vehicles.

The change in the moisture content of the air is also an interesting result of the cold. The air is really dry. That, combined with the cold, makes interesting things possible. The first is the miracle of the disappearing water. When it hits 30 below or colder, you tell the kids to take a cup of really hot water and throw it in the air. So you take the water and pitch it up into the air AND IT DISAPPEARS. The vapor pressure difference between the hot water and the air is such that it all evaporates. BOOM! A puff of steam and it's gone. Now hurry back into the house before you freeze.

The miracle of freezing breath is also pretty neat. The water in your breath freezes. If you have to walk far, the air that goes out of your mouth and by your head freezes in your hair. I have a beard and the air freezes my breath into ice balls that gather in my beard and become quite substantial. When it gets really cold, colder than 35 below, you can HEAR the water freeze as soon as you breathe it out. It sounds like little bells: the snow fairies.

Speaking of snow fairies, we also have snow snakes and whiteouts. The scientific name for a snow snake is actually saltation of snow. To explain a snow snake, I need to back up just a bit. You can get what is called snow creep, snow saltation and the worst, snow suspension. In snow creep the snow is pushed along by the wind. In snow saltation, the wind moves the snow right along the ground/snowpack/road. As it is blown along, this snow just sort of hovers a very short distance above the ground. This saltation is usually in swirling patterns and can blow a fairly long way over smooth surfaces (roads, frozen lakes, packed snow). Saltating snow usually looks like a snake moving along the ground. It is actually very neat. Snow snakes and snow creep move most of the snow. But the worst is suspension, known as whiteouts in bad cases. Whiteouts, also called turbulent suspension, happen when a lot of snow goes into the air due to wind. This can limit visibility to feet or even inches. I have been so confused during intense whiteouts that, when walking, I did not know which way to go. I just stood still until they cleared. If you are driving on the road, these can be deadly. If you are driving during an instant white out, you have no choice but to continue driving (slowly), watch the fog line on the road and hope that some idiot doesn't stop in the road ahead of you.

Frostbite is another constant friend. As I was often in the field during the winter while I was in Minnesota, the question is not really if you got frostbite this past winter. It was how many times you got frostbite. To be honest, the dangers of frostbite might be a bit overrated (or I might just be lucky). I have had parts of me freeze (tips of fingers, one of my cheeks, an ankle, bottoms of earlobes, a patch on my knee, a toe) and have warmed them quickly, like you are supposed to, and then worried. So far, none of them have come to anything really bad. I have lost the feeling completely in the toe that froze. For about a year, I had no feeling in the side of my thumb, but eventually it returned. One of my ankles turned really dark and has stayed that way (this one worried me the most). But nothing has developed gangrene or fallen off, like you hear in the old stories. I guess I have been lucky, but it is just about impossible to live here and work outside without a bit of frostbite.

SADS (seasonally altered depression) is another winter-related friend. The sun rises at the end of December at 7:00 AM and sets at 4:30 PM. I leave for work at 6:45 AM and leave for home no earlier than 5:00 PM (usually much later). If I am inside all day, I see the sun for 15 minutes to a half hour in the morning and that's it. If I am outside, the angle of the sun is really low on the horizon, so I hardly get any sun. By the end of winter, I have gotten very pale. I honestly did not know that I could even GET pale skin, but I did out here. My wife, who does have pale skin, begins to glow. And that is when the SADS sets in.

Exposure to light is a basic human need. Something about the lack of light triggers a psychological response that is like a mild (or in some cases more severe) depression. Some people are more susceptible than others. I have only suffered from one case and cabin fever shares part of the blame (which you will read about a little later). That winter started with a late October snowstorm that did not melt until early May. During the middle of that winter, I would look at the thermometer every morning. If I saw it as high as 15 below, I knew it would be a warm day. It did not rise above zero for six weeks. That year, I experienced a case of SADS. I knew what it was and I was worried. I was so desperate to get past it that I turned on my brooder lamps (light used to keep baby chicks warm when they are little) and lay down on the floor under them. Believe it or not, it helped a lot. Humans have a psychological need for light. Without it, we go a little weird.

For outdoorsy people, winter can be a blessing or a curse. I like to snowshoe and cross-country ski, which helps. Other people like to ice fish or snowmobile. Hunting is also a big sport but is mostly over by the depth of winter. But into the months of January, February and parts of March, it is often too darned cold to do much outside except ice fishing and sledding (sledding out here means snowmobiling). If it is a brown winter, cold with no snow, the world is lost. During these brown winters, we don't even get normal snow. We get SNIRT. Snirt is windblown dirt from the open plowed fields that combines with whatever snow we get and blows. This is the ugliest, messiest stuff that you can imagine. In the snirt winters, there is not much to do outside. Most winter activities require snow. Besides outdoor activities, there is nothing else to do in small northern Minnesota towns. To quote the billboard advertisement, "After all, beer freezes." I will skip this story, however. In summary, these brown winters, the winters of snirt, lead to horrible cases of CABIN FEVER.

For those that have not had a case of cabin fever, you really need to experience it in order to understand its effects. It gives you an excuse to be grouchy, antsy, and depressed all at the same time. Couples that live through a few northern Minnesota winters and are still together truly love each other. They have doubtlessly seen the worst of the other person and have nothing really bad left to see. A May to November romance (one of a young person and a much older person) can take on a bit of a different meaning when you consider cabin fever. I will relate a bit of a cabin fever entrée served with a side of SADS and intense cold to illustrate the point. All parties, including my wife, will remain nameless to preserve their anonymity.

This family lived in a small town in North central Minnesota. They were a loving family of four: a mother, a father, a son and a daughter. They loved the outdoors and gardening. By the time the first fall frost burnt down most of the garden in mid-September, they had frozen or canned quite a lot of produce. They had a pig and some chickens in the freezer and eight cords of wood cut, split, and stacked. They had saved some fresh greens under plastic in the garden for fall soups and salads. By late October, the first big snowstorm buried the world. On Halloween kids wore snowshoes and costumes over parkas. The snowshoes were a cute addition, not really necessary, but cute. After all, it was early in the season and the snow was going to melt. We might as well enjoy it while it lasted, right? It lasted until May.

Early winter went well, and the snow was great to play on. Every week or so a big blizzard dumped at least another foot on top of the old snow. This was great. The husband needed the exercise and went out and scraped the drive and sidewalks. And every week the piles of snow grew taller. The snow was deep enough that I made, I mean, the husband made, a tunnel network for the kids to play in. There were snow forts and snow piles high enough to use as sled runs. The family burned wood for heat and the house was toasty warm. They ate like kings. Renditions of songs with verses like "stoke the fire, read a book, give the storm another look…" kept popping into his mind. It was beautiful.

About the end of December, the place kept getting colder. It never rose above zero from the end of December until mid-February. Even then, it only warmed up to something like two or three degrees. When it bottomed out, this family could do nothing to keep the house warm enough. They were burning enormous fires, 24 hours a day, and the house would not stay warm. The air that drafted up the chimney stack drew in air from outside that was SO COLD that even a blazing fire was not enough. The husband and wife would get up a couple of times at night and feed the fire. They would save huge, dry oak and elm logs to put on at night to keep the fire as long as possible between feedings. The gas furnace was set to light at 50 degrees, and the thermostat was in the room with the fire. The rest of the house was colder. Every night at about 2:00 or 3:00 AM, the furnace switched on.

They decided to move everyone into the room with the wood burner to sleep, because the rest of the house was darned cold. And for this winter, eight cords of wood was not enough. As the snow deepened, more and more of the wood pile was unrecoverable from underneath the snow. The woodpile had to be dug out as did everything else. By the end of January, there was nowhere left to put the snow. The piles had to be lifted, which means that the lower levels had to be scraped and put on the top of the piles. This requires carving steps into the side of the pile and climbing them with each shovel full. The piles at the end of the drive really climbed high. A 20-foot tall red maple was planted there. The husband set a goal to fully bury the tree, and by the end of March, it was gone.

By the end of January, the desperate situation with the fuel supply became obvious. This winter was going to be a bad one. The family had enough wood for a normal winter, but this was abnormal. Thus began the desperate search. Permission was gained to cut from a brush pile on the research farm that the husband worked at. The chainsaw had to be kept in the cab of the truck to be kept warm enough to start. The first day, the temperature was 19 below when he cut wood. Most of the wood was frozen. He sharpened the chain every 15 minutes or so, because the ice and imbedded dirt in the wood had dulled it that badly. He cut only half a cord that day. It was an amazing accomplishment. More trips were needed, so he cut a truckload every evening after work before it was too dark to see. He cut until everything but the twigs were gone.

The individual pieces of wood were covered in ice and snow. It had to be brought into the house to melt before it could be burned. This was a mess. But at least the firewood cutting/scrounging got him out of the house. After the brush pile was finished, he no longer had a reason to be outside. Then cabin fever began.

Cabin fever is an interesting ailment. You see, everyone knows that a person has it except for the person with the affliction. Indeed, most of the afflicted believe that it is the UNAFFLICTED that are acting strange. If the case is so bad that the AFFLICTED recognizes it, it has gotten to the point of borderline psychosis. The husband recognized the affliction in himself as well as in his spouse. They must get out of the house and do something...anything.

The first choice may have been the most stupid one: a morphed version of outdoor winter racquetball/tennis. Go to the snowed in tennis courts and try to hit the ball around in 15 below weather and in parkas on a snow covered court. They truly were idiots.

The second choice was also stupid: outdoor basketball. This went a little better. The court was also a parking lot and therefore scraped of snow. The problem was that the basketball actually BROKE. The rubber that the ball is made of gets quite cold and fragile. A basketball is not made to dribble at 15 below.

The third idea was to drive out to the lake and have a picnic. Sure it was frozen, but they would have a chance to get out of the house, not to mention it would look beautiful. So the van got stuck and they were $60 poorer for the tow truck that pulled them out.

All-wheel drive only works if any of those wheels actually touch the ground. Boy the snow was deep that year.

The next idea was to go outside and roll snowballs and build the snow train. Building a snow train had been tradition in this family forever. Problem: really cold snow (air temperature less than 15 below) does not make snowballs, and snowballs are necessary to make a snow train. They ended up digging a channel around a roughly square area, making a seat and calling it a snow train. This one didn't fail, it just didn't work. But they had fun, sort of.

The last idea was the best: the daddy dogsled. You see, the husband needed to get some exercise badly, basically do anything physical. So he built a strong wooden runner dogsled out of oak scrap wood. He made it just big enough for two little kids and put a long set of lashings on it so he could pull like a dog. He then went and scraped a couple of hundred feet of sidewalk down to an ice base. He put the kids on the sled and away they went. It was great. It worked so well that he ran them to a convenience store about a half-mile away and bought hot chocolates. Cabin fever was on its way out.

Winter lasted for almost two more months. The snow started early and ended late. That's when the husband grew so desperate for light that he laid down under artificial lights. Cabin fever can be pretty harsh.

Cities on Ice

Winter runs an awful long time in the Upper Midwest. In my prairie home, road parking snow restrictions go into place at the end of October and are removed at the end of May. That is seven months of potential snow. After the lakes freeze up in early December, until the legal icehouse removal dates (March 15th at my prairie home), little cities of ice fishing shacks spring up on the lake.

Ice fishing is a big sport in Minnesota. Some cities number in the hundreds or even thousands of houses. Streets are plowed just like city streets. In some places they even put up street signs so that you can find people's icehouses (or your own). Some ice houses are as large as normal houses. Most are the size of small cabins. Some are highly mobile and able to occasionally move to follow the fish. Some never leave the original drop spot. But all have one thing in common: they protect you from the elements. And they contain beer, lots of beer.

Ice fishing, for the uninitiated, involves auguring a six or eight inch hole in the ice and fishing through it. This is not the kind of fishing that you do in summer. In winter, the action is very slow and most species of fish bite pretty gingerly. Fish are cold blooded after all, and it is just a couple degrees above freezing.

While the opportunity to get into the outdoors in winter is great, the practice of ice fishing is somewhat less appealing. You go fishing in the great outdoors without any shelter and freeze. The fetch, which is the open area upwind of a location that allows the wind to gather speed, can be quite long on a lake. Trees, shrubs, and grass slow down the wind. Lakes have none of these, so the wind just wails. The normal temperature might average up to ten degrees below zero. The real cold days may reach 42 below zero. The wind stings like a lash when it hits you. Except on really warm days (like ten degrees above) or those with abnormally still air, this is just unpleasant. Thus the fish house and truck fishing were created. The fish house, a stationary structure, creates part of a little village. Truck fishing is like an icehouse with an engine. You drive around drilling holes as you go and when you find a good spot, you fish out the door of your truck while sitting on the truck seat. If you are smart, you park the truck with the driver's side downwind, making a built-in shelter. This is the state sport of Minnesota for most of the winter.

Dairy Farms and Cheese

It is hard to talk about natural resources in Wisconsin without mentioning dairy cows and cheese. According to the Wisconsin Dairy Industry, Anne Pickett opened the first cheese factory in 1841. From that humble beginning, the dairy industry expanded. Currently, Wisconsin producers make two billion pounds of cheese a year, enough to sell every person in the United States seven pounds of cheese a year, once again according to the Wisconsin Dairy Industry.

While driving the Wisconsin landscape you will see fertile (and not so fertile) pastures dotted with black and white Holstein cattle eagerly eating grass and making delicious milk. As often as not you will miss cattle that eat in confinement facilities with all of their feed brought in to them. This presents a very different picture than the one on the label on your block of cheese. Most cheese labels show a cow in a meadow eating grass. Both of these types of dairy operations have an immense impact on the Wisconsin environment; however, the impacts of these two types of operations are very different.

"He leads me into green pastures…" is the quote from the Bible to describe the feeling of security and satisfaction of needs that a shepherd supplies to his flock. Green pastures are a sign of health and prosperity. They also contribute to a healthy environment.

Quality pastures with heavy grass cover can absorb nearly as much rain as a forest. This leads to less flooding and better use of the rain by the plants. Few nutrients escape from underneath a sod cover. The water that filters through a quality pasture and into the water table is usually of high quality. The plants harvest and use almost all the nutrients from the manure or fertilizer applied to the fields leaving clean water to percolate through the soil, at least on well managed pastures. Grazing is generally good for the water quality. None of this can be said about croplands.

Generally, ten times as many nutrients leach below row crops (like corn and soybeans) managed with best management practices (BMPs). Those given excessive nitrogen contribute to even greater leaching. The common practice of applying insurance nitrogen, which ensures that the crop has more than enough nitrogen available in case of excessive leaching conditions (like springs with heavy rains), results in dramatic increases in nitrogen export to the groundwater. The water that percolates to the groundwater in spring is loaded with nutrients that are great for plants but terrible for ground water. The loss of nutrients to a field is amplified even more if that field is tiled.

Tiling a field means adding subsurface drain lines that help water to leave the fields quickly in spring. This allows seasonally wet sites to be planted earlier in spring. It also allows soils that are always wet to be planted at all. For years, drainage was looked at as a good thing because people were taking waste land (swamps and low meadows) and turning them into some of the nation's richest farmland. Only recently have people started to reconsider the practice.

With increased drainage came increased peak flows of streams. Peak flows are the highest levels that streams reach when flooding. As these streams join into rivers, peak flows can become enormous because all these streams are dumping water in fast and furiously. This leads to terribly destructive floods. After seeing several 100 year floods, which reach a level seen every 100 years, I have decided that what was once considered a normal peak flow has changed. Agricultural drainage has increased them.

Pastures usually do not need to be drained. While drainage allows us to plant crops in seasonally wet fields in spring, most grazing lands are seeded very infrequently (or not at all) and therefore have fewer problems with early season high water. These fields can be harvested by grazing or haying to make cattle feed. With the grass cover, the peak flows are lower and the nutrients leaching into the ground water are reduced. This is good for everyone: farmers, consumers, adjacent landowners and even the cows.

For many years, the push was to increase use of confinement dairy farms. Farmers cut forage and hauled it to the cattle. They used corn as a cheap component of feed, a source of energy in the form of carbohydrates. With this change and the advent of BST/BGH, a pharmaceutical used to increase milk production, average milk yield for a herd of dairy cows went through the roof. At the same time, farm profitability went down and the farmer's free time disappeared. While dairy farming has always been time intensive, the extra time (and expense in machinery and fuel) needed to cut feed and haul manure every day reduced free time to a minimum. Many dairy farmers never take more than an hour or two of time off... ever.

With grazing, the herd average milk yield goes down because there is less energy in grass than in corn, but profitability usually goes up because there is less equipment and fuel to buy. Farmer free time also gets a drastic upgrade. Generally, cows live longer, as there is less need to cull (sell for slaughter) unhealthy cows. Because the cows live longer, they produce more calves (and milk) during their lifetimes. The state average annual cull rate is 37% according to a grazing specialist in North-central Wisconsin at a grazing field tour I attended but grazers may have a rate of less than 15%. Grazing farms produce more calves and need fewer as replacement animals. This provides another profitable income stream: calves for sale as replacement animals for confinement facilities. If you only need to replace 15% of the herd each year, you can sell 85% of the calves. With almost 35% of the total leftovers being heifers (young female cattle), which are often worth several hundred dollars as calves, it is easy to make this a good sources of income. For confinement facilities, replacing 37% of the cows every year means that they produce very few extra heifers for sale. They do sell more old cows but at a much lower price and with much higher costs. Grazing wins again.

As more and more of Wisconsin's small dairy farms go bankrupt, mainly due to poor economies of scale and while California adds dairies (mostly of enormous size with economies of scale that allow confinement facilities to win out economically), the impact of dairy farming on the local economies and culture in Wisconsin is diminishing. For the remaining dairy farms, the size and use of confinement facilities is increasing. These decisions change the nature and environmental impact of dairy farming. Plus, the picturesque landscape of Wisconsin seems vacant without the grazing cows. Wisconsin is the dairy state after all.

Hazelnut and Burr Oak

The land burned here often years ago
Plants that sprout new tops from old roots
And those with thick bark
Are all that are tough enough to survive.

Burr oaks always seem ancient,
Large spooky branches,
Enormous broad crowns,
Gnarled old trunks

As a seedling, they may sit for 50 year
Building large roots but only a tiny top
Waiting around in the grass and wildflowers
For a fire to burn and make them sprout,
An ancient baby tree.

Ancient hazelnuts,
With 1000 year old roots,
With tops growing old and diseased
Until fire starts them anew and fresh.

Only in recent years
Have the red oaks and maples come
Fires left them no more than small trees and shrubs
Until the world changed, white settlers came and ended
the fires.

How different a place looks full of so many trees
That nearly no light reaches the ground
So full of trees that the grasses have died and
Prairie flowers have gone away

Most oak openings are gone now
Savannas of a few trees and shrubs and a lot of grass
Replaced by forests full of trees
A changed world.

Even before I knew what the words
"savanna" or "oak openings" meant, I knew that I loved
that ecosystem. Oak openings, or savannas, are areas of
the country where fire, grazing, or soil conditions reduce
the number of trees below the level that would make a
full canopy over the ground. These trees often have
large low limbs and have grown in open conditions for
most of their life. Savanna can have as few as a couple
of trees per acre or have as much as half of the ground
covered by trees. But a savanna always has enough
open land for other plants to dominate on the ground.
While the trees are the obvious ones, the grasses, forbs
(wildflowers) and legumes are the "dominant" vegetation.

I saw these ecosystems as a child all over the
mountains. Areas that had cattle or sheep pastures
usually had a few trees and some resistant shrubs.
Areas on top of mountains that used to burn often had
old stately trees, a few shrubs, and a lot of wildflowers.
I thought these were the most beautiful landscapes I
had ever seen.

I particularly remember two of these
"savannas" on the way to my grandmother's house.
The first had scattered, ancient, open-grown oak trees
and a dug pond. This field fed cattle at one time, but
for most of my childhood, it stood idle. The field grew
goldenrods and black-eyed Susans, and Joe-Pye Weed
grew around the pond. The trees were always full of
birds, too far away to see. The birds were so numerous

that they looked like swarms of bees. It was beautiful. Now, the field grows an industrial park. A building sits where the old pond was. The black-eyed Susans and goldenrod only live in my memory, superimposed on top of mowed bluegrass.

The second savanna was actively pastured, and as far as I know, still is. It sat on a cleared hillside with clusters of trees and shrubs surrounded by open ground. Looking at the trees, it was obvious, even from a distance, that they had been hit by lightning more than once. Some were basically hulks of what appeared were ancient trees at one time. Once again, the birds swarmed everywhere. I imagined that I could see the whole world from the branches of these trees, but it was the farm of a person that I didn't know, so I never climbed the trees.

The state I live in now, Wisconsin was once host to over a million acres of oak openings. Old white and burr oaks have bark that can resist fire. Young ones resprout from the roots after fires kill the tops. They are well adapted to this ecosystem. Hazelnuts are so adapted to this burning regime that they tend to become overgrown and diseased without it.

Black and red oaks do not live as long or tolerate fire as well, but they re-sprout beautifully. In places with frequent fire, they turn into trees that are not much more than shrubs. After years of burning and resprouting, a seedling turns into a "grub." A grub is nothing more than a root system with a large knob of woody tissue on top built for no other purpose than making buds and new shoots. The early settlers fought these grubs for years. After much of the cleared land was abandoned, the grubs turned into trees and the battle was lost. Most of these abandoned farms are now forests. The farms that remained inhabited finally killed out the grubs, leaving open fields. Nearly none of the actual oak openings exist in their former condition anymore. They have all naturally or unnaturally converted to something else.

It is important not to forget the grasses and wildflowers, the dominant vegetation of savannas. The shade from the trees and the full sun in the open areas produces an incredibly diverse community of plants. Plants that normally only survive in the shade of forests (wild geraniums, columbines, ramps) can thrive in savannas, living under the trees. Plants that normally live in prairies (bergamot, blazing star, big bluestem, leadplant) survive very well in savannas. Some species (certain asters, wild lupins and others) specialize in savannas and grow very few other places. Individually, most of these species are not that rare; however, savannas are the only places that have these species assembled together.

Two things conspired to change these ecosystems from savannas to forests: the loss of fires and the intentional conversion of the land to other uses. Fire was an early enemy in this country. Prairie fires and forest fires threatened lives and properties. Natural and accidental fires were put out regularly once the land was platted out and the settlers established themselves. The previous fire regime present in these savanna ecosystems was largely anthropogenic, meaning of human origin. The Native Americans used fire as a management tool. Many oak openings areas were a result of the intentional action of the Native Americans who managed them.

Without this anthropogenic burning and with the settlers' constant battle against natural fires, the forests changed. The grubs sprouted to trees and these trees began to dominate the sites. Many of our forests of white, black, and red oak are the remains of ancient white oak savannas with a lot of overgrown red and black oak grubs. The grasses and wildflowers have changed creating a very different system.

Many of these savannas have also been intentionally converted to other uses. Oak savannas on richer soils have become much of the prime farmland in Wisconsin. Oak savannas on poorer soils that have not already grown into oak forests have often been converted to pine plantations. In this way, one of the most widespread ecosystems in the country has become one of the most endangered.

Monarda, Liatris, False Indigo and Bluestem

Around the ancient oaks
A sea of rippling grass stretches
Out to the horizon at the top of the hill,
And disappearing over the other side.

Monardas and liatris bloom every year,
In wetter years, bluestem, with its tall turkey foot
seed heads
Sends its seed to the wind,
In drier years, the gramas with their short one-sided
seedheads win.

Closer to the ground,
Violets of many types, red sorrels, wild onions
Fill the spaces
That the grasses and wildflowers missed.

Armies of ants, with their laundry basket-sized hills
Legions of immigrant worms and small mammals of
every sort,
Churn up the earth
One tiny piece at a time.

An awfully busy place
For a small patch of grass between the trees.

Native Americans made many of the savannas
across the Upper Midwest. Open savannas responded
well to burning allowing for foods such as raspberries,

blackberries, blueberries, currants, gooseberries, grapes, hazelnuts, liatris and oaks to thrive.

Wild blackberries and raspberries bear fruit on two-year old wood. Older patches of berries get to be overgrown with unproductive wood. They are hard to harvest and they get diseases. Burning eliminates the old and diseased canes, refreshing them so that they bear heavily in the second year after a burn.

Burning of lowbush blueberry patches has an even more dramatic impact. Low bush blueberries bear the heaviest two to three years after a burn. These plants are easier to harvest. Overgrown blueberry plants have crooked stems and lots of dead wood. A blueberry picker has to pick one berry at a time. However, young plants off of old roots have straight stems. You can use blueberry rakes, a box with closely spaced tines (almost like a fork with dozens of teeth), and pick dozens with each sweep. Each sweep of the rake grabs the plant and removes the berries from the plant. One person using a blueberry rake on vigorous 2-3 year old plants will pick as many berries as 10-20 people picking on old plants in the same amount of time.

Hazelnuts and oaks also benefit. After a fire, hazelnuts will often produce shoots nearly as tall as the old plant during the first year. These shoots have little disease. Most of the disease is eliminated by the fire and will take years to build up. Most of the weevils which feed so heavily on hazelnuts and oaks are also killed. Within two years, the hazelnuts bear again. Usually, the first crop after the hazelnuts have been coppiced (had their tops removed and resprouting initiated) by fire will be a very large one free of insect damage. The oak trees that bear for the first couple of years also get the benefit of reduced insect damage. As both acorns and hazelnuts were a highly desirable source of food (rich in protein and fats), this is an important impact for the harvesters.

Even currants, gooseberries and grapes are impacted. While I don't know that fire increases the yield of currants, gooseberries or grapes, it does refresh the stands and keeps them from converting to forests.

Fire also keeps the trees widely spaced. These widely spaced trees grow large crowns and can live a long time. Large crowns and older trees (150 years plus) mean large numbers of acorns in a concentrated location: a benefit for wildlife and human harvested. Trees that can tolerate the repeated fires (burr and white oak) flourish in this environment.

The soil also changes. Soils in forests are covered with leaf litter and rotting wood. Most of the organic matter produced during a year in the forest stays in the trees where most of the nutrients are locked up. Some trees or branches die and fall. As stands age and volume of wood in the stands increases, the soil nutrient level can decrease just because these nutrients are tied up in the trees (at least in ecosystems where nutrients are limited). Of course, the leaves and some needles fall every year. But for the most part, much of the organic matter remains in trees. This means that most forest soils have a thin layer of humus enriched top soil. The soil in savannas differs from this. Most of it resembles grassland soils. If the soil is loamy, the top 12 or more inches might be dark black topsoil. If the soil is really sandy, it may well look like little more than a sandy beach with some plants growing out of it, quite different from forest soils.

Savannas are also loaded with herbaceous plants. Grasses, like big bluestem, little bluestem, Indian grass, side oats, switch grass, quack grass and brome, are common. Naturalized, but non-native grasses are also everywhere. Orchard grass, timothy and reed canary grass can dominate sites. However, the forbs (plants that most people call wildflowers) are the most impressive. Savannas have far richer communities of forbs than do prairies. More than a hundred forbs are common in savannas. Monarda, Liatris, goldenrod, asters, coneflowers, St. John's wort, milkweed, butter and eggs, and many others create a forb community that is nearly continuously blooming for much of the summer. Many have food or medicinal values. Monarda, Liatris, various sunflowers, mountain mint, milkweed, wild onions and pineapple weed all have food uses. These same plants as well as some of the asters, some of the coneflowers, leadplant, St. John's wort, catmint, bluestem and others have medicinal uses. Overall this system flourishes in the producing food products.

The disturbance regime that keeps these sites so diverse also leaves them subject to invasive weeds. The scourge of spotted knapweed, buckthorn, autumn olive, Russian olive, honeysuckle, barberry, wild parsnip and many others is hard to overestimate. Savannas are particularly subject to these weeds because of the frequent disturbance regime needed to keep them from converting to forests and because of the amazingly diverse ecosystem (more niches for different species). Many oak openings are so infested with invasive species that there is little room for the native species that normally occur there. For the few oak openings that remain in a healthy ecological condition, invasives will alter their function greatly.

In the end, humans decide how a landscape is maintained. The oak openings, themselves, are of Native American origin. Managed by humans for up to 10,000 years (when the glaciers finally retreated in Wisconsin), these systems were maintained as a sort of forest garden. The trees and shrubs produced copious quantities of food with limited maintenance needs. Many of the herbaceous were useful for food and medicines. This provided an "economically" viable system for a culture that needed food, medicine, and game to be available in a low maintenance system. These systems may no longer match our societal needs or at least how we perceive our needs. The oak openings, a managed system of food and fiber production, have been replaced by corn, soybeans and pasture, resulting in another food and fiber production system. Doubtlessly, these new systems produce larger quantities of food and fiber, at least in the short-term. The glitch in the system is that row crops require much upfront investment and significant investment in planting, maintenance and harvest. They also vary greatly in production due to variation in weather, particularly rainfall. It is yet to be seen whether this system, in the long-term, is more economically viable than the savannas, as a food and fiber producing system. With the production of hazelnuts, cane fruits, acorns, and game that I have seen even during drought years and the desperate condition of corn yields during the same year, I have my doubts about the long-term potential of corn and beans (at least in this landscape, Iowa is a different story). The main arguments for maintenance of savanna ecosystems are usually presented as ecological; however, I believe that much of the "economics" of the systems have not been investigated fully.

What It Means To Be A Pig...
Or A Yellow Birch...
Or A Person

A few years ago, I read an article on growing hogs in hoop house structures instead of in hog confinement facilities. The article detailed economic and infrastructural differences and other things of interest to those wanting to grow hogs. One thing stood out to me in that article, something written almost as an aside. It stated that hog behaviorists have found that hogs need three things to be "happy" that lack in confinement facilities. These items prevent the animals from exhibiting negative behaviors such as cannibalism and fighting. They need a place to run, a place to burrow or root, and something to chew on (not just to eat but to chew). In other words, these things are what make a pig a pig. Thus began my family's saying: "That's what makes a pig a pig." When these things are lacking, the animal is in distress. When present, these things define the character of the organism.

Life is interesting. As I write this, I work as an Associate Professor of Forestry at University of Wisconsin-Stevens Point, a far cry from the hills in West Virginia and still quite different from working as an Extension Forester in Minnesota. But, it is interesting how everything a person has done makes a person what they are. It is like a long, very weird thread that goes this way and that, like a seam sewed by an 8-year-old: the little things that make each person unique. A friend told me a story originally told to her by an Ojibwe beader. When a person beads, if they notice that they have picked up the wrong bead and beaded it, they should leave the "mistake." This mistake gives the piece character, a life of its own, different from the 100's of other creations that could have been. Just like the little "faults" that make a person also give them character and make them lovable.

Today, I took a group of students out for class to use compass and pace techniques to mark out the boundaries of the 40 acre parcels that they would use for the next six weeks of classes. With the compass, the students find the direction of the property line, and the pacing measures the distance, an old but surprisingly accurate forestry technique. I dropped off the last group at one of their corners and began my walk back to the bus where I would wait for them.

I had a headache building all day, probably due to the intense effort of the forestry version of boot camp and partly also due to lacking sleep. I needed relief. I was grateful that I had seen a yellow birch on the way to the plots.

Yellow birch is a tree that grows on richer soils across much of the Northern states and follows the Appalachian Mountains down into and past West Virginia. The tree itself is reasonably intolerant of shade and can not start rooting into leaf litter, so you will see it growing in odd places. Often it starts growing on boulders or stumps or logs. As it grows, it drops its roots over the side of the stump and into the forest floor. These roots continue to grow as the stump or log rots. Eventually, these trees are suspended over bare ground by "stilt roots" where the stump used to be. The seeds of the yellow birch are borne in a type of cone structure. In winter the seeds of yellow birch often blow apart after good solid snow storms, especially those with heavy winds. The seeds blow across the wind-packed snow as one way of dispersal and come to land on another log or stump to start as another seedling. Often when I am out in winter I enjoy watching these seeds blow along as they become little seed snow balls: a very unique sight.

While all of these things are neat, I know this friend for another reason, methyl salicylate. You see, back to my headache, a number of species contain salicylates: willows, some birches and teaberries. Yellow birch particularly, with its wintergreen flavor, contains enough to act as a pain reliever. I was grateful to see my friend on the walk.

I cut off a small branch and as I walked back to the bus, I stripped the outer bark and ate the inner bark, like I was eating a long skinny ear of corn with really tiny kernels. In fifteen minutes or so, my headache was fading.

How do these things relate—hog behavior, me as a professor, birch growing on stumps and my headache? Over the years I have spent a lot of time looking at plants: as a kid, as a student and as a professional forester. While I appreciate everything that I learned about plants as a student and a professional by listening to people and reading, I really learned the most just getting to know what it "meant to be that plant."

For most plants (at least those around where I have worked), I recognize them and may know a bit of their life history. I may be able to relate some words in biology or ecology to them: early successional or late successional, subcanopy or herbaceous, euri or steno species. I may be able to use them to assess site quality. However, they are more like acquaintances or casual friends. I know them and know a bit about them, but that is it. I don't know the little misplaced beads or the little miracles inside them that make them special.

Yellow birch is one of a few dozen close friends. I know their personalities, some of the little miracles and misplaced beads that make them into them: the defining characteristics that make a pig a pig. They are a part of the thread that makes me into me. And thankfully, at least in the case of yellow birch, they helped me with my headache.

My "Mountain Farm" in Wisconsin

I was in the Yucatan in Mexico about three years ago. That is a strange way to start a section about my farm, but bear with me. Merida, the big city of the Yucatan, is a beautiful and very safe city, nonetheless a city. With the exception of the architecture (y que todas personas hablan en Español), it is hardly any different from any other city across the world. There are still rich and poor, still educated people with high-paying jobs walking around with laptop computers and cell phones, still people that can't find jobs and live in cramped, dilapidated buildings or on the street, still traffic and air pollution, still tourists walking around and businesspeople running between appointments; a city, like New York or Chicago or any other metropolitan area. It is really neat, but I wouldn't want to live there. I am so glad that I got the chance to see the rural areas around Merida or I never would have seen the resemblance to West Virginia.

The little villages that I went through in rural Yucatan reminded me of the mountain "hamlets" in West Virginia. Chickens were running around the homes and many had makeshift henhouses. A hog or two lived behind many of the houses. Little stands along the main roads sold vegetables. Cornfields a quarter or half an acre lay here and there. Stone fences and half-clothed kids ran around. People grew home gardens with fruit trees. Despite the different fruit trees than in West Virginia, it looked like home.

I now live on a small farm in Wisconsin. We raise eggs, broilers, lamb, meat rabbits, hogs and vegetables for sale. We only sell retail. We produce exceptional quality and sell for a bit more than you pay at the grocery store. If I cannot GREATLY EXCEED the quality that most people routinely buy, I will not sell the product. I will either use it myself or feed it out to the hens or hogs. Take my eggs as an example. My eggs are never over four days old. The groceries are allowed to sell them for 90 days. The hens are fed forages and lower quality garden vegetables (although many times these vegetables are higher quality than those from a grocery), cracked grains and oyster shell (for good egg shell strength) in addition to the regular layer ration. The Omega-3's (the good fats in foods) are doubtlessly higher in these eggs than those from the grocery. Research shows that hens raised this way produce eggs that are better for you. This is not a big surprise. The yolks are darker due to the vitamin D in the vegetables that the hens eat and the flavor is far superior. The hens are raised with a lot of space and fresh bedding. They are happy hens producing an exceptional product. Of all the products that we produce, I am the most proud of the quality of my eggs.

On this farm, I follow a combination of guidelines from the French food quality principals of Label Rouge (although I cannot sell under this name as it is trademarked), the conservation ethic behind sustainable agriculture, and the common sense behind a mountain farm. Each item of food sold from the farm is produced to the highest quality of flavor without damaging the environment. We sell food, after all, not an industrial feedstock, like #2 yellow field corn.

We generate few waste products. Basically, we look at nothing as waste. Damaged vegetables provide hog or hen food. They will take what they want out of it and turn the scraps to fertilizer. This fertilizer will be used to make more vegetables. Old baling twine is new ties for tomatoes or any of a hundred projects. Other peoples' old windows or siding or pallets find a home on some farm building project. Cardboard from old boxes becomes mulch. Shredded office paper can be animal bedding and then with addition of manure, fertilizer. You name it and we may be able to put it to a good use.

This farm had not been worked for several years before we bought it. The landowner was a nice fellow that had wanted a place out in the country, not really a farm, just a piece of land. After a divorce, he wanted to get rid of the place. The house is a bit less than 100 years old. The barn was built in 1915. While the previous landowner had put some work into the place (primarily the second floor of the house), much of it needed repair. To put it another way, EVERYTHING needed repair. I will be fixing things for the next 10 years, things that three owners back should have fixed. I will also UN-fix some things that a couple of owners back fixed poorly. This is a pretty daunting task. But as I write this, I am in the middle of putting some of the property back into working land. It is looking pretty good so far.

Most farms now are called "agribusinesses" and farmers are now "agribusinessmen/women." This farm is far from an agribusiness and I am not an agribusinessman. Agribusiness describes what happens to farms when they follow the motto "get big or get out." The ones that survive the effort of "getting big" turn into agribusinesses…in other words those that can service the loans. Those that can't are forced to sell out (or are sold out by the lenders). We do not own an agribusiness. We are what is meant when people say the word "farmers."

Right now, my wife is a part-time farmer and full-time stay-at-home mom. She is also a trained plant biologist (BA and MS). I can't think of a finer use for those degrees than as a farmer. I am a part-time farmer and full-time college professor in natural resources. I can't think of a much better way to keep me in the "real world" of natural resources than vaccinating sheep or building fence.

As far as the farm loans aspect of agribusiness, I have a mortgage. I don't have loans on equipment. Because I farm on such a small-scale, what I can not do by hand, I do with used equipment bought WITH CASH. In all of these senses, I run a mountain farm.

As far as running a mountain farm out in the Upper Midwest, we will have to give it a few more years to see whether it makes sense. It will take a good 10 years to get the place into the condition that I want it and to start making enough money to be "a going concern." But in the meantime, it does seem to be going well.

Cornerstone Press

CEO: Dan Dieterich
President: Donna Collins
Corporate Secretary: Christine Mosnik
Editor-In-Chief: Peggy Farrell
Associate Editor-In-Chief: Andrew Ilk
Managing Editor: Ryan Ostopowicz
Associate Managing Editor: Trina Olson
Business Manager: Tara Cook
Production Manager: Sara Jensen
Designer: Joy Ratchman
Associate Designer: Colin McGinnis
Marketing Manager: Chuck Zoromski
Advertising Manager: Michael Philleo
Publicity Director: Amanda Fisher
Associate Publicity Director: Felicia Ciula
Associate Publicity Director: Chris Warren
Sales Manager: Dale Bratz, Jr.
Substance Editor: Maggie Hanson
Associate Substance Editor: Jennifer White
Copy Editor: Nelson Carvajal
Associate Copy Editor: Aimee Freston
Associate Copy Editor: Ingrid Nordstrom
Associate Copy Editor: David Stelter
Associate Copy Editor: Daniel Henke
Fulfillment Manager: Andrea Vesely
Webmaster: Jason Roskos